A DOCTOR'S REUNION

LAURA SCOTT

READSCAPE PUBLISHING, LLC

 Created with Vellum

1

Flight Nurse Kristin Page was seated in the Lifeline staff lounge, cradling a cup of coffee and scrolling through a website on her phone searching for an affordable apartment, when she was distracted by a deep male voice.

"Krissy? Krissy Page? Is that you?"

Krissy? No one had called her Krissy since her dreadful high school days. *Prissy Krissy.* Ugh. She glanced up with a frown, then paled as a blast from the past hit her squarely in the face.

Holt Baxter.

"W-what are you doing here?" she sputtered.

Holt was as tall as she remembered, with wavy dark hair and the all-too familiar mesmerizing green eyes. A nanosecond later, she realized he was dressed in a one-piece navy-blue jumpsuit.

Just like hers.

For a long moment, she couldn't breathe. Holt worked here at Lifeline Air Rescue? How? Why? Since when?

"I'm one of the new residents assigned to the Lifeline

rotation." He smiled warmly, approaching her as if they were long-lost friends instead of enemies. "Wow, it's great to see you again."

No, it wasn't. There was nothing great about it, at all. She felt a flush of embarrassment creeping up her neck toward her face. Her gaze darted around, seeking an escape route. But of course, there wasn't any way to avoid the inevitable. Finally, she blurted, "No one calls me Krissy. My name is Kristin."

His green eyes widened, and his smile faltered. "Oh, okay. Sorry about that. I'll do my best to remember."

Mortified at her behavior, she wanted to curl into a ball and disappear from sight. What was wrong with her? That fateful day at Carlson's Custard had been nine long years ago. Another lifetime, really. So what if his younger sister, Heidi, had humiliated her in front of Holt? Her ridiculous crush didn't matter after all this time.

She was a different person now.

And Holt was different, too. Apparently, he was an emergency medicine resident, soon to be a successful doctor. To say she was surprised was an understatement. Not that Holt hadn't always been smart, because he was. But she'd never heard that he'd gone to medical school. Seeing as she'd worked critical care at Trinity Medical Center, she was grateful they hadn't crossed paths before now.

"I'm impressed you're a flight nurse," Holt went on. "Very cool."

Was that a subtle reference to the fact that she'd been anything but cool during high school? She knew only too well that she'd been the chubby girl with thick glasses and braces who had never been as popular as his beautiful sister, Heidi.

A fact Heidi and her mean-girl cheerleader friends had mercilessly plagued her with on a regular basis.

Stop it. She was being ridiculous. Nine years ago, remember? She forced a smile. "I'm actually fairly new here, just started a few months ago."

"Really?" He looked relieved. "Then maybe we can learn together. I've gone through the training program Shelly O'Connor provided, but this is my first flight. I have to say it's pretty intimidating to think about providing care miles in the air with no way to get additional help."

"Yes, it can be challenging, but it's exciting, too." She tilted her head to the side, regarding him thoughtfully. Holt sounded sincere and not the least bit arrogant, the way some residents were. Was it possible he'd forgotten about what happened nine years ago? As soon as the thought entered her mind, she rejected it.

No way. He was just being nice, acting as if they were friends back then rather than two teenagers who'd once worked the custard stand together until she'd been called out as a love-sick moron in front of him. She knew full well it was no coincidence he'd quit his job three days after the incident.

"It will be fun to fly with you." Holt's comment startled her. "You were always calm and cool under pressure."

Huh? What in the world was he talking about? The only pressure they'd been under back then was when their local sports games had ended and the mass of spectators mobbed the custard stand for a post-game treat. Maybe they had worked together just fine, before Heidi had humiliated her, but still. From what she could tell, Holt was taking the whole *we had fun times together* pretense a bit too far.

"We'd better head in to get the report from the off-coming shift." Kristin set her coffee aside and moved to push up off the sofa. Holt rushed forward to offer his hand.

She hesitated, then accepted his unspoken offer, knowing it was better to remain polite and cordial since they'd be working together. His fingers were warm around hers, and a shiver of awareness rippled up her arm.

Oh boy. She pulled away as soon as she could, hoping Holt hadn't noticed her involuntary reaction to him. Bad enough that she'd had a huge adolescent crush on him nine years ago, but now? Uh-huh. No way. Not happening. She refused to be stupid enough to repeat the mistakes of her past.

Guys like Holt Baxter were so not her type.

"Thanks." She hurried toward the debriefing room.

"Kris-Kristin, wait. You forgot your phone."

She glanced over her shoulder, nonplussed to realize he was right. Her phone with the rental site app was still sitting on the sofa cushion where it had dropped from her nerveless fingers. Holt picked it up and brought it over to her.

"Apartment hunting?"

"Um, yeah." She didn't plan to elaborate on the fact that her fiancé had left her several months ago and living in the same oak Terrace apartment building shared by Greg and his new girlfriend had become intolerable. She took her phone and entered the debriefing room. Their oncoming pilot, Nate Landry, was already there, along with Reese Jarvis, the off-going pilot. Another resident she didn't recognize was seated there, a pretty blonde who reminded her a bit of Holt's sister, Heidi, and Ivan Ames, one of their long-time paramedics.

"Hey, Kristin," Ivan greeted her. He was happily married with a young daughter, and the most cheerful guy she'd ever worked with. "Oh, and you must be Dr. Baxter." Ivan rose and offered his hand. "Nice to meet you."

"Call me Holt." Holt shook hands with Ivan and the two pilots. He nodded a greeting to the blonde. "Hey, Paulette. How are you?"

"Fine." The blonde's tone was clipped, making Kristin wonder if they had a history of some sort. She wouldn't be the least bit surprised to find out that Holt Baxter left a trail of broken hearts in his wake.

Including hers.

"Any transfers pending?" She looked at Ivan and Nate since Paulette was staring down at her phone.

"Nope. Weather is good, sunny and warm for October, so no incoming storms to worry about either." Ivan waved a hand. "We had a transfer from Plymouth earlier in our shift, then an early call for a car versus tree. Otherwise, it's been quiet."

"Sounds good." She glanced again at the female resident. "Anything to add, Doctor?"

"What?" The blonde glanced up in annoyance, then shook her head. "No. If that's all, I'm heading home. Good night."

"Good night, Dr. Yost," Ivan said.

Paulette Yost. The name didn't ring a bell, but Kristin knew it was her own fault for not paying closer attention to the new batch of residents that had just come off training. If she'd bothered to look at the list more closely, she'd have noticed Holt Baxter's name and wouldn't have been caught off guard by seeing him again.

And now she'd be flying with him.

The entire mood in the room lightened after Paulette Yost left. After they chatted for a few minutes, Ivan sighed and rose to his feet. "I need to get outta here. Hope you guys have a good shift."

"We will." She infused confidence in her tone, despite her misgivings. "Sleep well and give your daughter, Bethany, a kiss for me."

Ivan's grin widened. "I will. Good night."

"I need to get home, too." Reese rose to his feet. "Gabe hasn't been sleeping well, and I know Samantha is exhausted."

Reese Jarvis and his wife, Dr. Samantha Jarvis, had welcomed a baby boy a month ago. Gabriel Jarvis was adorable with red fuzzy hair just like his mother's. Sam brought him in for a visit, and Kristin had held him close, battling a wave of sadness in knowing motherhood was far out of her reach. Her destiny was to live alone.

"Now what? We just wait for a call to come in?" Holt asked.

"Yep." She dropped into the seat across from Nate. "You may as well help yourself to coffee or tea. Waiting is the hardest part of the job."

Holt hesitated, then shrugged and made his way back into the lounge where the coffeepot was located. She leaned forward and dropped her voice so Holt wouldn't overhear.

"What's up with Dr. Frost?"

"You mean, Yost?" The corner of Nate's mouth quirked in a lopsided smile. "She got airsick. Ivan was a good sport about it, but she still got upset when he tried to give her advice."

"Ah." She could understand; the first time she'd flown, her stomach had turned upside down, too. "Well, I'm sure she'll get over it."

"Maybe." Nate lifted a shoulder. "If she's smart, she'll

follow Ivan's advice and take Dramamine prior to her next shift."

"She will. She didn't strike me as the type to appear weak in front of others." She shrugged, straightened, and changed the subject. "Sounds like Reese and Sam are doing well."

Nate nodded. "Yeah, they are. I need to check on the bird. Mitch was tinkering with her earlier, and I want to be sure there's nothing to worry about."

"Let me know if there's a problem. We have to notify the paramedic base if we can't fly."

"Will do." Nate disappeared out to the hangar.

Kristin sat for a moment, dreading the idea of going back into the lounge with Holt.

Flying with him would be torture enough, but sitting and chatting about the past?

Yeah, she'd rather have hot needles poked into her eyes than endure that.

HOLT BAXTER SIPPED HIS COFFEE, reeling from the idea of working alongside Krissy Page.

He remembered her well, a bit geeky, as he'd been, but easy to work with as they'd served countless cones and dishes of custard throughout the summer.

Too bad his sister Heidi had poked her nose in where it didn't belong, ruining their friendship. After the scene in the custard stand, he'd felt bad he hadn't had the chance to talk to Kristin about it. It had been mid-August, and he'd already given his notice as he was moving into the dorms of the University of Wisconsin in Madison to attend college.

He hadn't spoken to Krissy—no, Kristin—until now.

"This is a three-month rotation for you, isn't it?" Kristin crossed over to retrieve her cup, then refilled it with coffee from the pot. He noticed she drank it black, the way he did.

"Yeah." He eyed her over the rim of his mug. Kristin hadn't changed much, other than getting contacts and having her braces removed. She wore her walnut brown hair longer now, the glossy strands pulled back into a thick ponytail, her eyes a mixture of green and gray and brown. She'd grown into a beautiful woman, although he'd always thought her pretty and hadn't understood why Heidi had decided to pick on her. "Honestly, I was glad to get the fall rotation rather than the winter one."

"Trust me, it will still be winter in November and December."

"True. But the weather always turns far worse after the holidays."

"Yeah, I have to admit, flying in the summer is much nicer than flying in the winter."

"I bet." He inwardly winced at the inane conversation. He wanted to bring up what happened at the custard stand but sensed she was avoiding the topic.

"You graduate in May, don't you?"

"Yeah, I can't wait." He grinned. "It's been a long road, and I'm glad it's almost finished."

"You like emergency medicine?"

"Of course. There's always something new coming through the doors. And what about you? Where did you work before coming to Lifeline?"

"In the surgical intensive care unit at Trinity."

He tried to hide his surprise. "Really? I had no idea you were a critical care nurse there."

"Yeah, well, it's a big hospital with lots of employees."

She looked down at her pager as if she might be willing the stupid thing to chirp.

The atmosphere in the room went tense, and he knew they couldn't ignore the past for a moment longer. "Listen, Kristin, I wanted to apologize for my sister . . ."

Beep! Beep! Beep!

"We have a call." Kristin's expression was relieved as she removed the pager and read the message. "A trauma alert, looks like someone jumped or fell off the roof of Greenland High School." For a moment their gazes locked, and he knew they were both remembering their time together at Brookland High. "I'll grab the supplies, and we'll meet Nate out at the chopper."

Kristin hurried over and looped a large black duffel bag over her shoulder. He kept pace alongside her. As she headed through the debriefing room, she stopped long enough to grab a helmet, before walking out to the hangar. He took a helmet too and tried to keep a neutral expression on his face, despite the fact that he was internally grappling with the idea of going to the scene of a possible suicide.

It wasn't his first suicide patient, and since he'd chosen a career in emergency medicine, it likely wouldn't be his last. This type of scenario shouldn't catch him off guard; this kind of thing happened far more than it should. Yet each time he was faced with a potential suicide victim, he relived those dark days just over a year ago, after his sister's attempt to end her life by downing vodka and a handful of narcotics.

All because she'd found out her perfect life with her perfect husband hadn't been so perfect after all.

"She's ready to fly," Nate said as they approached.

"Good." Kristin opened the door and climbed inside the helicopter. Holt followed, pulling the door shut behind him.

As they took their seats on either side of the gurney, he

donned his helmet and tried to remember everything that Shelly O'Connor had taught him. There were controls on the seat handles to open communication channels between the flight team and the paramedic base. He also knew it would be a smart idea to get some sort of basic information from the emergency medical team at the scene.

Kristin began jotting notes on a clipboard. Holt watched, feeling more than a little useless. Determined to do his part, he flipped the intercom switch. "Base, this is Dr. Baxter, requesting an update from the scene at Greenland High School."

There was no immediate response. Kristin glanced at him, then reached over to flip the switch adjacent to the one he'd used. "This is the all comm," she told him. "Now you're connected to the paramedic base."

He told himself it was an honest mistake. He repeated his request and this time received a response.

"Lifeline, this is the paramedic base. Patient is a fifteen-year-old male, unconscious at the scene with several broken bones, including spinal and head injuries from falling off the roof of the school. Vitals are not stable, and the paramedics on scene have been performing CPR."

"Ten-four." He flipped off the intercom to the paramedic base, leaving just the internal one on, and glanced at Kristin. Her expression behind the face shield of her helmet was grim. "Doesn't sound good."

"No, it doesn't." She paused, then added, "Nate? What's our ETA?"

"Less than five minutes."

Holt took a deep breath and let it out slowly. The ride would be much longer if they were in an ambulance, but knowing the paramedics were performing CPR, even five minutes seemed interminable.

He peered through the window, searching the scene below. Even from up here, he could see the flashing red lights of the ambulance and at least three police cars parked in the front of the school.

Hurry, hurry, he mentally urged Nate. Holt couldn't shake off the lingering fear that despite the quick flight, they would arrive too late to save this young boy's life.

Kristin felt tension radiating from Holt in waves, filling the small, cramped interior of the chopper. She wasn't sure if it was related to this being his first flight. Or something more. As an emergency medicine resident, this couldn't be his first trauma patient.

As Nate landed the helicopter in an open area of the high school parking lot, she quickly disengaged from the communication system and jumped out the side door, hurrying around to the back hatch. Holt had followed her, and between them they pulled the gurney out, snapped it upright, and jogged over to where the ambulance was parked.

She had to remove her helmet to hear what was going on. The resuscitation efforts by the paramedics on scene were still going strong. She knelt on the opposite side of the young man's body and felt for his carotid pulse, catching the gaze of the paramedic performing chest compressions.

"Good pulse with CPR. Hold for a moment, let's see what rhythm he's in."

Holt crouched next to the paramedic giving breaths with a face mask. "I'll intubate him."

"Hang on for a minute." She was watching the heart monitor positioned at the kid's feet. "Looks like we have asystole. Let's continue CPR, I'll take over the compressions."

The paramedic nodded and sat back on his heels. "We've been at this for close to fifteen minutes. It's not looking good."

She nodded, understanding what he meant. Fifteen minutes was a long resuscitation considering there was no underlying cardiac issue that could be reversed. Asystole meant his heart was completely stopped. After fifteen minutes of being down, all the drugs and compression efforts in the world wouldn't make this kid's heart start up again.

"We have to keep going." Holt's expression was full of grim determination.

"We've given epinephrine several times, along with running fluids wide open. We've also infused two units of O neg blood without a response," the paramedic pointed out. "And we don't have any idea how many fractures he's sustained."

"Check his pupils." Kristin knew that if this kid had a severe intracranial bleed, there would be no way for him to survive their resuscitation efforts.

After a long moment, Holt said, "Both pupils are fixed and dilated."

Her heart felt heavy as she looked at the teenager's face. She hoped and prayed that he hadn't jumped to his death. Not that simply falling on his own was any better, but an accidental fall might be easier for his family to face than a suicide.

She continued doing chest compressions, waiting for Holt to call the code. Physicians had the ability to stop resuscitation efforts, but nurses and paramedics didn't. Unless of course they reached the point of sheer exhaustion.

Holt knelt beside the patient, staring down at his young face.

"You gotta call this one, Doc," the paramedic finally said. "There's nothing more we can do."

Holt looked up at her, and she nodded in agreement. He blew out a breath. "Stop CPR. Time of death zero eight thirty-five."

Kristin moved away from the young man's body, feeling sick and helpless. They'd done their best, had come to the scene as quick as humanly possible, but the end result was the loss of a teenager.

This was the most difficult part of the job.

"We'll transport him to the medical examiner." The paramedic glanced at her, then at Holt. "Thanks for your help."

"Worthless as it was." Holt's tone was bitter.

"Hey, we can't save them all." Kristin put her hand on Holt's arm. She was a little surprised he was taking this young man's death so hard. Holt was in his third year of the emergency medicine residency. Surely he'd had experience with other young patients who didn't survive.

"I know." Holt stared down at her hand for a long moment, then met her gaze. "Let's get out of here."

She nodded and picked up her helmet. Holt did the same, and they wheeled the gurney back to where Nate waited with the chopper, the engine still running. They donned their helmets, stored the empty gurney in the back, and climbed in.

"Base, this is Lifeline, returning to the helipad," Nate

said. "Patient declared deceased at the scene."

"Ten-four, Lifeline. You're clear to go."

Holt didn't say anything on the short ride back to Lifeline. She felt bad that his first flight had resulted in a poor outcome. But that wasn't necessarily unusual. For every ten flights they did, one or two would result in a less than positive outcome.

When they were back in the lounge, she offered a wry smile. "Hey, I'm sure our next flight will be better."

Holt nodded, dropping onto the sofa with a heavy sigh. "I hope so."

Despite their history, she found herself moving over to sit next to him. "Your first suicide?"

"No." He scrubbed his hands over his face. "I've had several, but the young ones tend to hit me hard."

She waited for him to elaborate, but he didn't. She told herself that Holt's personal life was none of her business. "I can understand that."

He didn't say anything more, so she took the hint and dropped the subject. Pulling out her phone, she went back to apartment hunting. Her lease was up at the end of October, and she really wanted to find something.

The sooner she moved away from Greg and his new girlfriend, the better. She currently lived in the older Oak Terrace apartment complex that was located just a few blocks from the Lifeline hangar, but there were new apartments that had gone up in the past few years at a complex known as the Crossroads. The only problem was that they were more expensive than her current place.

Still, it might be worth an extra two hundred a month to avoid Greg. Especially since the blonde bombshell had already moved into his place. Clearly, he'd started seeing Blondie while they were still engaged.

Whatever. He wasn't worth her tears. In fact, she should have figured out something was up, the way he'd grown distant. She'd thought it was the stress of planning a wedding. It hadn't occurred to her that Greg had found someone else.

Call her clueless in Brookland.

"Will we be able to find out what the cause of death is?"

Holt's question pulled her from her thoughts. "Um, yes, we can get a copy of the ME's report. It takes time, up to ninety days to get the toxicology screens back, but the preliminary report should be available in a couple of days."

He nodded. "High school sucks."

His comment surprised her. "Yeah, it sure does."

"I'm sorry." Holt turned to face her. "Heidi shouldn't have embarrassed you like that."

Embarrassed wasn't the word she'd have used, but she shrugged and strove to sound as if she couldn't have cared less. "It's okay. I'm just sorry you had to quit your job over it."

He frowned. "What are you talking about? I didn't quit Carlson's Custard because of Heidi's theatrics."

Why, oh, why hadn't she kept her big mouth shut? Talking about that night wasn't part of her plan. "It's not a big deal, but I know you stopped working there three days later."

"I had already put in my two-week notice because I was scheduled to move into the Madison dorm that following weekend." His gaze sought hers. "You really thought I quit over the things Heidi said?"

Yes, she had. Although, looking back, she could see that the timing of his going off to college made sense. She hadn't been able to go to a four-year college right away, choosing to attend a junior college for the first two years because it was cheaper and she could commute from home. Of course, Holt would have attended the more prestigious University of Wisconsin–Madison.

Still, he'd never once tried to talk to her after Heidi's humiliating announcement. Not that she could blame him. "Well, it's no big deal. Let's just forget about it, okay?"

He hesitated, looking uncomfortable. She stood and made her way over to the coffee machine. Desperate to change the subject, she asked, "You interested in another cup of coffee? I'll make a new pot."

"Sure."

She busied herself with making coffee, keeping her back to Holt as she tried to process what he'd said. Not only had he apologized for his sister's cruel remarks, but he'd basically reassured her that he hadn't left the job at the custard stand because of the incident.

Clearly it was time for her to let it go. What did it matter if Heidi had called her names and blurted out her secret crush? What seventeen-year-old girl didn't crush on an older guy?

She stiffened when she felt Holt come up to stand behind her. Her breath caught and strangled in her throat when he cupped her shoulders in his hands.

"I'm sorry about Heidi, but please know, I didn't leave because of it. If you want the truth, I was flattered."

Flattered? No way. She refused to turn around, staring instead at the way the coffee dripped into the pot.

Drip. Drip. Drip.

"I feel bad though. It wasn't nice of the other kids to laugh at you."

Ya think? She closed her eyes for a moment, then abruptly turned, wrenching out of his grip.

"Flattered? Yeah, right. You looked at me with pity. And

you never told Heidi to stop it either. She stood there, calling me a four-eyed, pathetic loser who was hopelessly in love with her older brother, and you didn't tell her to shut up."

He looked surprised by her outburst. "I—I guess I should have . . ."

"Yeah. You should have. But I don't care, okay? That was a long time ago. Since it looks like we'll be working together over the next three months, let's bury the past and try to keep things professional between us."

Without waiting for him to respond, she disappeared through the lounge to where the restrooms were located. Entering the doorway of the women's restroom, she closed and locked the door behind her, then collapsed onto the commode.

She was an idiot to have lost her temper like that. Nine years, and suddenly she was the same pathetic loser Heidi had called out that day in the middle of the custard stand. In front of the cool kids, who'd all pointed at her while sniggering and laughing.

"Loser, loser, pathetic loser . . ."

The memory was burned into her brain, even now. She could smell the grease from the burgers, the milk from the custard. She could see the faces leering at her and remembered how she'd wanted to run far, far away.

She should have been immune to the memory by now. And she had been, until Holt had dredged it all up again.

Flattered? She didn't believe that for one minute. Holt was just doing his best to smooth things over, acknowledge their history and move on.

Something she should have thanked him for, instead of attacking him about it.

Whatever. Her pager went off, echoing loudly against

the tiled walls of the bathroom. She stood, washed her hands and face, then went back out into the lounge.

Time to grow up and move on. Now that the past had been aired, they could both forget about it.

Three months from now, she wouldn't be working alongside Holt Baxter ever again.

She'd survived four years of being belittled by the popular girls during high school, surely she could survive the next three months working with Holt.

HOLT READ the text message on his pager, relieved to see their next call was a typical trauma call, motorcycle vs. automobile. Not that injured motorcyclists were easy to deal with, but it was something familiar. He grabbed his helmet just as Kristin emerged from the restroom.

"Let's go." She brushed past him as if nothing had transpired between them, once again hurrying outside to where Nate was waiting for them beside the chopper.

This time he knew what to expect and quickly climbed in behind Kristin. When they were airborne, he requested an update from the paramedic base, using the correct switch this time.

"Two injured motorcyclists on scene, female with fractures along her right side, but it's the driver who has a fairly significant head injury. Paramedics are stabilizing him on the scene."

"Ten-four." Holt disconnected from the base intercom, then cued his mic and glanced at Kristin. "We can only take one patient, right?"

"Correct. Too much weight and not enough room to

bring them both. We'll take whichever is worse off, likely the driver with the head injury."

"That's what I thought." He found himself silently hoping, praying that this patient survived long enough for them to get him to the emergency department at Trinity Medical Center. At least that way he'd have a fighting chance at surviving this crash.

Thinking about their patient helped distract him from Kristin's outburst. He couldn't deny a flash of shame. She was right, he should have told his sister to shut up. He'd gotten so used to blowing Heidi's comments off that he hadn't even thought about sticking up for Kristin.

Looking at Kristin now, he knew she was a much better person than Heidi had been. Look what she'd accomplished. An amazing career as a critical care nurse and now a flight nurse. Really, Kristin had no idea how much better off she was compared to his sister.

Heidi was still trying to figure out how to move forward with her life after making so many mistakes.

He didn't remember looking at Kristin with pity. If anyone deserved his pity, it was his sister. Not Kristin.

The chopper banked to the right, then dropped down into the center of the interstate. A goofy grin tugged at the corner of his mouth. He'd often been on the other side of the road, watching in admiration as the Lifeline Air Rescue team rushed over to provide their expertise.

Now it was his turn.

Kristin jumped out of the chopper and hurried around the back. He felt certain that she wouldn't hesitate to pull the gurney out all by herself if he didn't come and assist.

They removed their helmets and ran with the gurney between them to where two paramedics were working on the prone figure of a male who looked to be in his early fifties. His name was Leo Campine, and he wore leather pants and vest, which helped protect him from a severe case of road rash. But he hadn't been wearing a helmet to protect his head. The paramedics had already intubated him, which was nice.

"How's his neuro status?" He knelt beside the paramedic.

"Pupils are reactive, but the left one is larger than the right."

"Turn off those fluids." Holt waved at the IV bag. "We need to keep him dry to prevent more brain swelling."

"How's his blood pressure?" Kristin connected their portable heart monitor to their patient.

Holt hesitated, realizing she was giving him a hint. If the guy's blood pressure was too low, decreasing his fluids might cause heart damage, making his concern about brain swelling irrelevant.

"Hanging at one hundred systolic," the paramedic replied.

"Cut the fluid rate in half," he amended. "Let's see how he tolerates it." Holt knew he owed Kristin a thank-you for helping to keep him on track. "Any other obvious signs of injury?"

"There's a bruise on the back of his head, and I think his right arm is broken as well. There may be other fractures along with internal injuries, too."

"We'll get Leo to Trinity Medical Center ASAP." Holt quickly listened to the guy's heart and lungs. The lungs on the left side were diminished compared to the right, possibly from a tension pneumothorax. "Hand me an eighteen-gauge needle."

"His pulse ox is dropping," Kristin said.

Holt didn't waste a minute. After splashing a bit of antiseptic on the left side of the guy's chest, he inserted the large-bore needle into the space between the fourth and fifth intercostal ribs. A whoosh of air came out.

"His pulse ox is improving, up to ninety-two percent now." Kristin gave him a nod of approval. "Ready to get him on the gurney?"

"Yes." Their patient was a large man, so it took all four of them to place him on the longboard and lift him onto the Lifeline gurney.

Loading him into the back of the chopper took additional muscle as well, and he couldn't help looking at Kristin with admiration. She was stronger than she looked, in more ways than one.

Once they had the gurney secured and they were settled inside, Kristin gave Nate the signal. "We're ready to go."

"Ten-four." Nate revved the engines and brought the helicopter off the pavement. "ETA to Trinity approximately ten minutes."

Ten minutes wasn't much time. He slowed the fluids, keeping an eye on Leo's blood pressure. When it began to drop, he had little choice but to increase the flow. "Give a dose of Mannitol."

Kristin reached into the bag of supplies and pulled out the medication. Once it was given, she glanced at him. "He'll likely need a urinary catheter."

"Yes, please insert a catheter, thanks." She was certainly on top of things; he couldn't have asked for a better partner on his first day of flying.

The ten-minute flight went by fast, and soon Nate was landing the chopper on the helipad of Trinity Medical Center. He hadn't requested a hot unload, but there was a trauma team waiting for them anyway.

Kristin rattled off their patient's vital signs as they

entered the trauma elevators. "Pulse tachy at one eighteen, BP hanging in at ninety over fifty. He's breathing a bit above the portable vent, which is a good sign, pulse ox steady at ninety-four percent."

"Tension pneumothorax on the left, likely right-sided brain injury," Holt added.

"We'll get him into the CT scanner stat," the trauma surgeon agreed.

They reached the emergency trauma bay within minutes, and the rest of the team came to take over. They slid him off the Lifeline gurney onto an ED cart, then Holt stepped back, waiting for Kristin to disconnect their portable monitors.

It wasn't easy leaving Leo Campine in the hands of the Trinity Medical team, but Holt knew their role in caring for him was over.

They quickly cleaned the gurney with bleach wipes from the ED stock, then headed back up the elevator to the rooftop helipad.

"Now that's what I call a successful transfer." He grinned.

She nodded, returning his smile. "Yeah. Nice job."

"Thanks to you." He searched her deep green-gray-brown eyes. "I appreciate the way you helped me out."

She blushed and turned away. "It's nothing."

It wasn't nothing, but Holt let it go. For now.

He was intrigued by the beautiful, confident, and intelligent woman Kristin had become. A woman he very much wanted to get to know better.

Yet she'd just told him they should keep their relationship professional.

Which was her way of saying she didn't feel the same way about him.

3

S pending thirteen hours with Holt was far more difficult than she'd ever imagined.

Not because he treated her poorly or looked down on her. Quite the opposite.

He hadn't hesitated to thank her for the subtle helpful hints she'd offered when he'd missed something and had often looked at her with admiration reflected in his green eyes.

She didn't get it. Where was the arrogance she associated with physicians? Wasn't Greg a perfect example? Sure, there were a few nice guys out there, but none who had ever treated her as sweetly supportive as Holt had today.

Maybe he was simply going out of his way to make up for the past.

By the time their shift had ended, her nerves were stretched as thin as piano wire. The nicer Holt acted toward her, the more difficult it was to ignore her attraction to him.

Why oh why hadn't she grown out of her teenage crush? Was this some sort of weird rebound from discovering Greg kissing Blondie one night five months ago when she'd gotten off early from her shift?

Kristin had no idea, but whatever these feelings were, she hoped she could find a way to squelch them once and for all.

"I'll walk you out to your car." Holt fell into step beside her as they left the Lifeline hangar.

"It's perfectly safe."

"Maybe, but it gets dark early these days."

"Thanks." He was so close their fingers brushed by accident. She eased away, hoping he couldn't see the erratic beating of her pulse. "When do you work next?"

"Tomorrow."

She hid a wince. Great. She was working, too. Another thirteen hours working alongside Holt. Just what she didn't need.

As they approached her ten-year-old Honda, she gestured toward it. "This is me. Thanks again."

"No problem." He stood, waiting for her to unlock the vehicle and slide in behind the wheel.

Feeling self-conscious, she lifted her hand in a wave. "See you in the morning."

A smile bloomed on his face as he understood they'd be working together. "Yeah, see you tomorrow."

Her fingers were clumsy as she put on her seat belt and started the engine. Holt didn't immediately leave but stood off to the side, watching as she backed out of the parking spot. Thankfully, there weren't many cars in the lot, so there was no danger of her hitting anything.

As she drove across the lot, she noticed a bright blue pickup truck. It wasn't something she would have thought Holt would drive, but she knew Ivan's black SUV on sight, and there was another small, sporty red car, maybe a Corvette.

Dr. Yost, aka Frost, was the likely driver of the Corvette. She told herself it didn't matter, but she still couldn't quite picture Holt behind the wheel of a pickup truck.

When she pulled into the parking lot of her apartment building, she had to admit that she may have misjudged Holt Baxter. All these years she'd considered him to be the male version of his sister, Heidi. That to him looks, popularity, finances, and prestige within the community were all more important than anything else.

Humbling to consider she may have been wrong.

Entering the building, she stopped short when she saw Greg and Blondie wrapped in each other's arms waiting for the elevator. They lived on the second floor, not too far from where her apartment was located, so their decision to take the elevator didn't make sense. Averting her gaze, she gave them a wide berth as she headed for the stairs.

"Kristin?"

Greg's voice made her wince. She glanced briefly over her shoulder. "What?"

"I'd like you to meet Wendy Sallinger, she works in the medical intensive care unit." He was acting as if they all might be good friends, hanging out together. "Wendy, this is Kristin Page."

To her credit, Wendy looked just as flummoxed as she did by the introduction. Maybe Greg thought this would make things less awkward. Yeah, so not.

"Hi, Wendy. You should remember that once a cheater, always a cheater."

Without waiting for a response, she hurried up the stairs, away from the two of them. Maybe saying her thoughts out loud wasn't very nice, but it was true.

Why would Wendy think that it was okay for Greg to cheat on Kristin with her yet believe him when he claimed he'd never do that again? It made no sense. Greg should have called off their engagement the minute he found himself attracted to Wendy. But instead, he'd lived a lie for weeks, maybe even months.

And she had no doubt he'd do the same to Wendy. Maybe not now, but someday, when someone younger, prettier, flashier, and richer came along.

Good riddance, she thought as she unlocked her apartment. Seeing Greg and Wendy up close had only reinforced how fortunate she was to have learned the truth before they married.

Now if she could find a new place to live and find a way to ignore her attraction to Holt, she'd be all set.

KRISTIN DIDN'T SLEEP WELL, she kept flashing back to her troubled high school days and the lengths she'd gone to avoid Heidi and her cheerleader friends.

Sticking her head in her locker, waiting for Heidi and her gang to walk past. Eating lunch in the bathroom or skipping lunch and raiding the kitchen to gorge on food when she returned home. Eating so much custard she'd grown sick of it. Kristin still couldn't go to a custard stand without feeling as if she might throw up.

The pretty blue pickup truck was in the lot when she arrived, but in a different parking space than the evening before. Definitely belonged to Holt. Steeling her resolve, she parked several spots away and quickly entered the hangar.

"Hi, Kristin." He greeted her cheerfully from his position near the coffeepot. "Coffee's almost ready."

"Great, thanks." When the pot was full, he filled two cups and handed one to her. She was surprised he'd noticed she drank hers black. She took a sip, then headed into the debriefing room.

Both Paulette and Ivan had worked again last night, and Reese had been their pilot. Reese's expression was serious, not necessarily unusual, but Ivan's scowl was an indication things hadn't gone well. Ivan could see the bright side of a dirty penny, so she knew without asking he was frustrated and angry.

"Hey, Ivan." She was afraid to ask how his night had gone. "Are you off the weekend?"

"Yeah." Ivan's tone was clipped.

Reese didn't say anything but glanced pointedly at Paulette Yost. The resident sat with her arms crossed over her chest in a defensive stance, her beautiful face held a bit of a sneer.

"Paulette, how did it go last night?" Holt's question hung in the air for a long moment.

"We had two transfers last night, we just arrived back from the second one," Paulette said. "Unfortunately, the patient suffered an in-flight cardiac arrest and didn't make it."

Kristin sucked in a quick breath, glancing at Ivan and then Reese. Losing a patient during a transport was a rare occurrence. Sure, they couldn't prevent every complication, but being prepared and planning ahead were two key elements that assisted in keeping their in-flight mortality rate extremely low.

"I'm going home." Ivan abruptly stood and left the debriefing room. Darting a quick glance at Holt, she hurried after him.

"Ivan, wait." She snagged his arm. "What happened?"

"Our patient needed to be intubated, but she kept insisting it could wait until we landed." Ivan jammed his fingers through his hair. "I tried to do it myself, but the guy was huge, and I couldn't see very well. Maybe that's why she didn't want to try, I don't know. But we lost his pulse ten minutes into the flight. We did CPR until Reese landed the bird at the closest hospital, but it was too late. The doc there pronounced him dead."

Her heart squeezed at what he'd gone through. "I'm so sorry. Maybe you should talk to Jared about this." Jared O'Connor, Shelly's husband, was the medical director of Lifeline Air Rescue. He was board certified in peds and adult trauma and still worked several shifts a month. "He needs to know about Paulette. Maybe she's not a good fit for this program."

"I left him a voice mail when we returned." Ivan shook his head. "The worst part? She wouldn't accept responsibility for her role in the debacle. If we'd intubated him right away, or if she'd at least tried, he might still be alive."

"I'll follow up with Jared, too." She offered a lopsided smile. "Get some sleep and try not to worry about it."

"I asked Jared if there was a way that I didn't have to fly with her anymore." Ivan grimaced. "Not that I think anyone else should be stuck with her."

"I'll talk to Jared," she repeated. "He'll pay attention to an in-flight demise."

Ivan turned away. Kristin blew out a breath and returned to the debriefing room. Paulette was coming out as she was going in. The female resident didn't acknowledge her in any way but simply left in Ivan's wake.

Kristin glanced at Reese. "Sounds like it was bad."

"Yeah." Reese wasn't the type to gossip, but it was

obvious he was troubled by what had happened. "I tried to reach Jared but got his voice mail."

"Ivan left him a message, too. Don't worry, he'll follow up with both of you."

"I take it losing a patient during a flight isn't a common occurrence?" Holt asked.

"No, it's not."

For a long moment no one spoke. There wasn't much she could do about Paulette Yost now. As much as she hadn't looked forward to flying with Holt again, the thought of being partnered with Paulette seemed far worse.

In fact, if she were honest, she'd admit she'd been looking forward to working with Holt again. Now more than ever since she knew Holt would do whatever was necessary to save a patient's life.

He was exactly the type of flying partner she wanted.

HOLT DIDN'T LIKE HEARING Paulette and Ivan had lost a patient, and he was more than a little curious about what had happened. He made a note to find out more from Kristin when they were alone.

"Where's Nate?" Kristin asked.

"I'm here." Nate entered the debriefing room. "Sorry I'm a few minutes late."

After a brief discussion about the weather conditions, Reese left. They'd barely finished their first cup of coffee when their pagers went off.

"Request for a transfer from Kenosha," Holt read out loud. "Fifty-two-year-old with severe pulmonary hypertension."

Kristin nodded. "Sounds serious, let's go."

They settled into a routine, Kristin taking the supplies and Holt following her into the helicopter. As Nate lifted them airborne, he communicated with the Kenosha hospital ICU to get an update on the patient's condition.

Holt didn't have a lot of experience with severe pulmonary hypertension, the only thing he knew was that the medication that was used to treat the disease had to run continuously without interruption. Stopping the medication abruptly could cause severe rebound pulmonary edema.

He'd witnessed firsthand how a patient had been literally foaming at the mouth when they'd arrived after the medication had run dry without a replacement being ready. Heaven knew he didn't want to go through that again.

The trip to Kenosha took a full eighteen minutes. When they reached the rooftop helipad, he and Kristin climbed out and wheeled the gurney into the elevator. The intensive care unit was located on the third floor, and they found their patient without difficulty.

"Dr. Eppers? I could use an update," Holt said as they approached.

"Patient is Arlene Jacobson, and she was recently diagnosed with pulmonary hypertension. We've done our best to stabilize her, but the expert on dealing with pulmonary hypertension is at Trinity Medical Center."

Arlene looked pale and thin against the bedsheets. He listened as Kristin introduced herself and quickly began switching over the equipment to their portable Lifeline devices.

She hesitated when it came to the IV pump. "Holt? Would you give me a hand?"

"Sure." He quickly came over. "What do you need?"

"I'm going to program this pump, then I need you to quickly disconnect that one and hand it to me. I'll have to change the tubing, which will take a minute, before I can reconnect it." Kristin began pushing buttons on their portable device.

"Maybe we should get another bag from the pharmacy." Holt didn't like waiting even a minute for the switch over.

"We can't waste it, it's super expensive medication," the ICU nurse protested. "And that's a brand new bag."

He decided to trust in Kristin's ability.

"Ready." She held up one end of the IV tubing.

He stopped the pump, quickly pulled the medication bag off the end, and handed it to Kristin. She spiked the bag, hung it on the pole, and quickly primed the tubing. Within twenty seconds she was reconnecting the IV line to the patient and starting the pump. "There. All set."

"Impressive." He grinned with relief.

"Her blood pressure is on the low side; we haven't been able to give many fluids." Dr. Eppers shrugged. "It's been a delicate balance."

"Understood. Is the feeding tube turned off?" Holt asked.

"Yes, for transport."

"Okay." Holt looked at Kristin. "Ready to get her transferred to the gurney?"

"Yes."

Ten minutes later, they were back on the rooftop. Holt helped push the gurney into the helicopter, then quickly joined Kristin inside. Nate waited until they were situated before getting permission to lift off.

Kristin placed the headphones on Arlene's head. "Can you hear us?"

"Yes." Arlene appeared calm, and he had to give her credit for taking this so well.

"Just relax, this will be a quick flight," he assured her.

They were only six minutes in when Kristin lightly touched his arm. "BP dropped to eighty systolic."

"Titrate up her maintenance IV fluids," he said. "But go slow, ten cc's at a time."

"Okay." Kristin did as he asked. He kept his eye on the monitor, there were no audible alarms, they had to rely on their eyes to keep track of what was happening.

Arlene's eyes drifted shut. He frowned. "Arlene? Can you hear me?"

No response.

"Arlene." He lightly shook her arm. "Open your eyes."

Still nothing.

"I'm going to check a finger stick," Kristin said, pulling out the meter. "Did you notice they only have saline running? No dextrose."

"Is she diabetic?" Holt asked.

"No, but her feedings have been off for a while, and one of the side effects of the medication she's on is low blood sugar."

It only took a few seconds for the meter to read a result, but it seemed like forever. "Glucose level is critically low at thirty-five."

"Give twenty cc bolus of D50." He wanted to give more, but he didn't want to cause a problem by using too many fluids. "Actually, give me the syringe of D50, you drop her IV rate down to where we started."

Kristin handed him the syringe and pushed the buttons on the IV pump. Within a minute, Arlene opened her eyes, looking around in confusion. Kristin rested a hand on the woman's arm. "You're doing fine; we'll be at Trinity soon."

"Thank you."

Holt looked at Kristin, their gazes locking for a long moment before she turned away. He turned his attention to finishing a quick assessment, as much as he could while in the helicopter. It was disconcerting not to use all his senses when assessing a patient.

"ETA eight minutes," Nate said.

Holt knew he wouldn't relax until they had Arlene safely transferred over to the emergency department physicians. Not having provider backup was the hardest thing to get used to, but he knew he was fortunate to have a nurse of Kristin's caliber to work with.

They made a good team. Back when they'd scooped custard together and again now.

Nate landed the chopper on the rooftop landing pad with a slight bump. Holt jumped out first, running around to the back to open the hatch.

Kristin pushed the gurney toward him from inside, then came out to join him. Two minutes later, they were in the emergency department.

From the corner of his eye, he noticed a pretty female resident with wavy auburn hair approaching on his left. His gut knotted when she spoke, the familiar sarcastic tone reverberating through him. "Well, if it isn't Holt Baxter."

"Lana." He did his best to ignore her, focusing instead on the attending standing to his right. "Ms. Jacobson is a fifty-two-year-old female newly diagnosed with severe pulmonary hypertension. During the flight, her blood pressure dropped and her blood glucose went down to thirty-five. We gave twenty cc's of D50, and she's doing much better."

"Sounds good. Dr. Pressio, the pulmonologist, will be here soon. He accepted her transfer but didn't have an ICU bed open, so we agreed to take her down here."

Holt nodded. "Call if you need anything else."

Kristin was helping the ER nurse reconnect the IV

medication, minimizing the amount of time it was disconnected. When she was finished, they moved Arlene onto the ER gurney and moved away.

"Paulette told me you're doing a Lifeline rotation, too." Lana appeared again, her gaze accusing. As if he'd taken her spot, which was ridiculous as to his knowledge she didn't even apply.

"Yeah, it's been great. Sorry, gotta go." He turned his back on Lana and caught Kristin's gaze. "Ready?"

Kristin arched a brow but nodded. They wheeled the gurney out of the emergency department. He didn't glance over his shoulder, but he could feel Lana's gaze boring into his back.

"Former girlfriend?" Kristin asked when they reached the elevator.

He hesitated, then reluctantly nodded. "Yes."

"Seems like she wants you back."

The idea was repugnant. "No way. She's too high maintenance for me."

"Really? I would have thought you'd be perfect together."

He frowned. Kristin's statement was hardly flattering. But there wasn't time to say anything more as their pagers went off. They wiped down the gurney with bleach, then stored it back in the chopper.

But as Nate flew them to their next destination, her words echoed over and over in his mind.

After breaking up with Lana, he'd felt lighthearted and free. It had taken him longer than it should have to realize Lana was too much like his mother and sister.

He knew now he'd prefer being with someone more casual, more down to earth.

Someone exactly like Kristin Page.

4

Of course, Holt would be attracted to a beautiful woman like Dr. Lana Reasby. She was attractive, smart, and soon to be an attending physician, just like Holt. What was puzzling was that the relationship hadn't lasted.

High maintenance? Like his sister, Heidi? She would have thought Holt would be used to that. Whatever. It wasn't any of her business. Holt wasn't her type. Okay—no doctor was her type, despite the weird awareness she felt every time he was near.

Her problem, not his.

All she needed to do was to survive the next three months and he'd be out of her life, forever.

They had several back-to-back calls that kept them busy. She was grateful for the chance to focus on patient care rather than being forced to endure idle chitchat.

And she really, really didn't want to talk about Heidi.

"Wow, is it always this crazy?" Holt wiped sweat from his brow. "Those helmets get hot."

"When the snow flies, you'll be grateful." She couldn't

help but smile. "But to answer your question, no, it isn't always like this."

Their pagers went off again, and she groaned. "Only an hour before the end of our shift, doesn't that just figure?"

"At least the hospital isn't far."

"True. Let's go." Kristin had just restocked their supplies, which had been dwindling as the shift went on. She threw the bag over her shoulder and headed out to the helipad.

"Hopefully the last call for our shift," Nate said dryly. "I'll need to refuel after this transport."

Kristin nodded and hiked herself up into the chopper. Holt joined her, and Nate went through the preflight checkoff before lifting the bird into the sky.

She listened as Holt received an update from St. Jerome's Hospital located ten miles west of Milwaukee. "Barbie Martin is a twenty-year-old female with severe malnourishment due to anorexia. Her vitals are relatively stable, but her electrolytes still need to be corrected. She's losing consciousness, but so far we haven't needed to intubate her."

"Okay, thanks for the update." Holt clicked off the mic, his expression grim. "I hope she makes it."

"She will." She infused confidence in her tone. It was difficult to comprehend starving yourself, yet at the same time, remembering the names she'd been called in high school, she could see how it might happen. Kids were cruel, and it wasn't until she'd reached college that she'd learned even the most popular kids were now green freshmen, just like the rest of them. Their former popularity didn't carry over to college.

She cast a sideways glance at Holt, wondering if he knew how Heidi had treated her nine years ago. When they'd been in elementary school, they'd been friends. But that all changed when Heidi became one of the high school cheer-leaders. By senior year, a tight group of cheerleaders followed Heidi around when she wasn't dating the high school quarterback. What was his name? Taylor? Tyler?

Nate banked to the left, his voice pulling her from her reverie. "ETA three minutes."

She finished documenting a few notes on her clipboard, then set it aside. She really needed to stop rehashing the past. As soon as Nate landed the chopper, this time on a surface landing pad, she and Holt jumped out.

They found the four-bed ICU on the second floor of the small hospital. As they entered the unit, she immediately noticed two parents hugging each other as they gazed down at their young daughter.

Barbie Martin didn't look twenty, she looked much older. She was gaunt, her skin pasty and thin, without much elasticity. Her blond hair was stringy and limp, her breathing labored. Kristin swallowed hard, acknowledging this was the worst case of anorexia she'd ever seen. And even more disturbing? They could try to fix the physical impact of what this girl was going through, but until Barbie received the mental health services she needed, this would remain a constant battle.

The doctor on duty approached Holt. Kristin listened as she connected Barbie to their portable equipment. "Her blood pressure has been hanging in the ninety over forty range. Her pulse remains tachy at one twenty. Respirations are twenty-four, and she's hypothermic at ninety-six degrees."

"We can use a blanket warmer during the transfer," she told Holt. "That should help."

"Is my baby going to be all right?" Barbie's mother asked, wringing her hands. "You won't let her die, will you?"

"We're going to get her safely transported to Trinity Medical Center." Kristin did her best to sound reassuring. "It's a short flight, won't take us long at all."

"Can I come with her?" The woman's swollen bloodshot eyes were pleading.

"I'm sorry, there isn't enough room inside the helicopter." She gently covered the woman's hand with hers. "I promise we'll take good care of your daughter."

Barbie's mother's eyes filled with tears, but she nodded and turned away, burying her face against her husband's chest. The couple looked helpless, and Kristin wished there was more she could do for them.

But getting Barbie physically stable was only a small part of the battle. She hoped, for their sake and their daughter's, they'd consider going into an intense counseling program.

Once she had the equipment ready to go, they moved Barbie onto the Lifeline gurney. Their heated blanket was in the helicopter, so they packed layers of blankets around her for the short trip outside.

Even though it didn't take long, Barbie was shivering by the time they lifted her gurney up and into the back of the helicopter. Kristin worked to get the heated blanket connected as quickly as possible. At barely ninety pounds, their patient couldn't afford to waste energy shivering.

When that was finished, she placed the headphones on Barbie's head. "Barbie, can you hear me?"

Her eyes remained closed, but Barbie nodded. Satisfied for the moment, she began charting vital signs.

"Kristin, I think we should change her fluids to Ringer's lactate solution. It might help correct her electrolytes."

"Okay." She pulled out a liter bag from their supplies and hung it on the IV pump. Fluids were clipping along at

150 cc's per hour through an IV in her subclavian vein, which should help keep her stable during the flight.

Out of nowhere, Barbie abruptly reached up and pulled out her central line. Bloody fluid spurted around the interior of the chopper as Kristin tried to shut off the pump. Holt put pressure on her chest where the catheter had been.

Barbie's eyes were wild. "I don't want IVs or feedings! I don't want anything! Leave me alone!"

"Restrain her arms," Holt said. Kristin was able to capture both of Barbie's thin wrists. "We need to replace that central line."

"Nooo . . ."

Kristin caught Holt's gaze. "Should we do that against her wishes?"

Holt's mouth thinned, then he nodded. "Yes, I think we should. I don't think she's in her right mind at the moment." Within seconds, Barbie's blood pressure began to drop. Her eyes fluttered closed. On the monitor, she began to have irregular heartbeats.

"Restrain her arms so she can't hit us." Holt's expression was grim. "I need to get this central line placed ASAP."

Kristin did as instructed. When he placed the catheter in the other side of Barbie's chest, she didn't flinch.

Her gut squeezed painfully.

They were losing her.

Beads of sweat rolled down her face. Kristin had the IV ready to go the minute Holt had it in place. She vaguely heard Nate saying something about their ETA being five minutes, but she ignored him.

Once the fluids were connected, she glanced at Holt. "Meds for her heart?"

"A bolus of amiodarone." As she reached for the medication, she heard him cue the mic. "Paramedic base, this is Lifeline requesting a hot unload."

"Ten-four, Lifeline."

Barbie began to struggle weakly against the restraints. "No. I told you no."

Kristin leaned down, capturing Barbie's gaze. "Barbie, do you want to die?"

"No."

"Okay, then you need those fluids to keep running. Without them, you'll die, understand? You will *die*."

Barbie closed her eyes and turned away. Kristin was relieved she'd stopped fighting, but she was still inwardly reeling from the close call.

Nate landed the chopper, and she waited for Holt to jump out first. She pushed the gurney toward him from inside, then came around to join him. They were met by a team of doctors and nurses from the emergency department. There was no way to be heard above the sound of the chopper, so they had to wait until they were inside the building to let the team know what had happened.

"Her blood pressure is still only eighty-four over thirty-six," Kristin reported. "Her pulse is also irregular and remains in the one twenties."

"Do you think she's decisional?" the ED attending asked Holt.

Holt hesitated. "I don't. I think her pulling out the IV was a symptom of her disease process. She clearly stated she didn't want to die, yet she also said she didn't want any fluids or feedings. You may need an ethics consult on this one, as she's twenty years old and normally should be able to make her own decisions."

The attending nodded. "Yeah, good idea. Thanks."

She and Holt accompanied Barbie to the ED's trauma

bay. After they moved her off the gurney, she quickly disconnected the equipment and piled it on top.

Holt stopped near a box of bleach wipes and helped her
clean the blood and fluids from the gurney, pumps, and
monitors. They'd have to clean the interior of the chopper,
too. "That was a close call."

"Too close," she agreed. "Not the best way to end the
day."

"I don't suppose I could interest you in stopping for a
bite to eat after work." Holt's tone was casual, but his gaze
was intense. "We didn't get much of a break today."

The idea of going out with Holt was so startling, she
tripped over her own feet, managing to catch herself before
she face-planted on the floor. "Oh, uh, I don't think that's a
good idea."

"Oh, I didn't realize you were seeing someone."

"I'm not." The denial popped out before she could catch
herself. "But I don't date doctors I work with."

"I see." He nodded, even though she saw skepticism in
his gaze. "Does that mean you'll have dinner with me after
my three-month rotation here is over?"

"Oh, uh, well, I don't know..." She couldn't seem to pull her
scattered thoughts together. Why on earth was he pursuing
her? The last thing she wanted to do was date another resident.

Greg Zeman had been bad enough.

"Think about it, okay?" Holt tossed her a quick grin, and
she found herself nodding.

"I will." Wait a minute, no she wouldn't. Dating Holt
wasn't ever going to happen. Not now. Not in three months.

Not ever.

She wondered if flying with Dr. Frost—er—Yost, would
be easier than fighting her attraction for Holt.

How in the world was she going to last the entire three months of working with him?

She had no idea.

HOLT COULDN'T REMEMBER the last time he'd been so quickly and thoroughly shot down.

He tried to shake it off. After all, hadn't he been enjoying his freedom after breaking up with Lana? It had been four months, and there was no reason to rush into another relationship.

But working alongside Kristin made him realize how important it was to have someone you trusted at your side. Someone you could depend on for support.

Someone you enjoyed spending time with.

When they returned to the Lifeline hangar and cleaned the chopper with bleach wipes, the night shift crew was waiting for them. Not Ivan and Paulette this time, but flight nurse Kate Weber and another resident by the name of Matthew Abbott.

"Hey, Holt. How's it going?" Matt asked.

"Busy." He dropped into the chair, feeling as deplete as if he'd spent the entire twelve hours running a marathon. "The last transfer was touch and go."

After he'd described their last patient, Matt and Kate both winced. "That's a tough one."

"Yeah." He glanced at Kristin. "At least I had a great partner."

Kristin blushed. "Anyone else would have done the same thing. Listen, I need to get home. Do you need anything else from me, Kate?"

"I think we're good." Kate waved a hand. "Go, I know it was a long day."

Holt jumped up from his seat. "I'll walk you out."

This time Kristin didn't argue, maybe because she knew it was a wasted effort. Granted, the Lifeline hangar was located in a decent part of town, but he wasn't about to let a woman walk in the dark alone.

"It's because of Heidi, isn't it?"

"What?" Kristin paused with her hand resting on the door of her car.

"I should have stood up for you that day. I'm so sorry I didn't. I wish I could go back and change things."

"I don't want to go back." Kristin opened the driver's side door. "And that's not why I said no. It's just—I'm not interested in dating a doctor. I've seen more relationships between doctors and nurses fail than succeed." She looked away, shrugged, and tossed her purse into the passenger seat. "It's nothing personal."

"I see." It sure felt personal, but he appreciated her honesty. "Okay, forget I mentioned it. Have a good weekend."

"You, too." Kristin slid behind the wheel. He stood aside, watching as she drove off, before heading over to his bright blue pickup.

He lived in the new Crossroads apartment building, located not far from the hangar. He tried to remember if he had a frozen pizza left in the freezer for dinner. He was starving and had hoped to avoid eating alone.

His phone rang as he popped the last pizza in the oven. When he picked up his phone, he winced when he saw Lana's number. "Hello?"

"Holt, it's Lana. What's going on at Lifeline?"

He scowled, hoping the pizza would cook fast. "What do you mean?"

"I just got off the phone with Paulette, she's been placed on probation. And she claims it's your fault!" Lana's voice grew louder as she talked. "What are you doing? Sabotaging my friends to make yourself look better?"

"Hold on, I had nothing to do with Paulette being placed on probation." Although he was secretly glad Jared had taken action. "Residents don't fly with each other, we fly with nurses and paramedics."

"I heard the paramedic she was assigned to was horrible. He was nasty and didn't have a clue about what he should be doing."

"That's not true. Paulette isn't giving you the full story, Lana, and frankly I don't see any reason for us to discuss it. I have to go."

"Wait! Come on, Holt. You must have some pull there. Can't you put in a good word for Paulette? It's not her fault she got airsick."

"There's nothing I can do. I haven't worked with Paulette, so I can't give her a recommendation. Goodbye." He quickly disconnected before she could say anything more.

It was interactions like this that made him thankful he'd broken things off when he had. Being alone was better than spending time with Lana.

After eating his pizza, he dropped into bed and slept. The following morning, he ate breakfast and prioritized his chores. Grocery shopping and laundry were both high on the list.

His apartment included a washer and dryer, which he liked. No more hunting for quarters to plug into a machine.

When that chore was done, he decided to hit the grocery store.

As he headed through the lobby on his way out to his truck, he stopped abruptly when he saw Kristin standing off to the side, talking to the manager.

"Kristin! Are you looking to move in here?"

"Holt." She looked flustered at seeing him. "Um, this is just one of the units I'm checking out."

"This is a great place, nice and quiet. You'd love it." He tried not to overdo his enthusiasm, although he couldn't deny the flash of longing that hit hard.

Seeing Kristin even on a casual friendly basis after his Lifeline rotation was finished would be easier if they both lived in the same building.

"We offer many amenities," the manager said, sensing a potential rental in the making. "There's a great room that can be rented out for parties, and each apartment has its own laundry facilities."

"Sounds great. Thanks for showing me the available units." Kristin edged toward the door. "I'll be in touch."

Holt stared after her as she hurried away. It occurred to him that he may have been better off if they hadn't run into each other. She might have signed a rental agreement to move in if she hadn't known about his living here.

Unfortunately, it was too late now. She'd never move here.

All because of him.

5

Kristin kicked herself for overreacting at finding Holt striding through the lobby of the apartment building she'd toured first thing that morning. She really needed to get a grip on her emotions. Okay, yes, he was a nice guy and easy to work with. But she absolutely did not want to date him.

And maybe if she told herself that a hundred times a day, she'd begin to believe it.

She sighed and ran her fingers through her hair. She'd liked the apartment in his building better than any of the others she'd looked at. And it was available immediately. But now she was in a conundrum. If she moved in, would Holt assume she'd done it to be closer to him? And even if he didn't think that, how would it be to watch him dating other women?

Moving into the Crossroads might be going from a bad situation to a worse one.

Maybe she should stay where she was. The rent was cheaper, and she was over Greg and Blondie, aka Wendy. Yet she hadn't renewed her lease, so for all she knew, her current apartment may already be rented to someone else.

Swallowing a groan, she returned to Oak Terrace and knocked on the manager's door. The squat round manager opened the door, peering at her suspiciously. "What's wrong?"

She forced a smile. "Nothing is wrong, Mr. Jenkins, I was just wondering if you'd rented my apartment out yet."

The guy's expression cleared. "Oh, yes. Everything is set, thanks."

Her smile faded. "I see. Are there other vacancies in the building? I was thinking of staying for another year."

Jenkin's eyes gleamed. "I have a two-bedroom available; it's three hundred and fifty more per month than what you're paying now."

Three-fifty more? It would be cheaper to move to the Crossroads. "Oh, I don't think that will work. Thanks anyway."

"Let me know if you change your mind," Jenkins called after her.

She lifted a hand, acknowledging she'd heard him, then reluctantly pulled out her cell phone. Time was running out. She'd have to take the apartment at the Crossroads or pay even more to stay where she was.

After she made the arrangements with the Crossroads manager to return earlier that afternoon to sign off on the lease, she silently prayed that her apartment would be located far away from Holt Baxter's.

She spent the next couple of hours putting stuff she didn't use on a daily basis into boxes. The apartment she was moving into was currently vacant, and she was hoping the manager might let her move in early.

It would be nice to move her stuff over the span of a

couple of weeks rather than doing everything in one weekend. She'd asked off work the last weekend of the month to move, but maybe she wouldn't need those vacation days anymore. If they hadn't been covered by one of her coworkers, she could easily pick them back up.

Better to work than sit around staring at her apartment walls. She loved to read, especially suspense stories, but there were times she'd have rather gone out with friends.

Unfortunately, the friends she had were all couples, people she and Greg had gone out with together. Now that she wasn't with Greg, she didn't feel like tagging along like a third wheel.

After eating a quick lunch, she put a couple of boxes into the trunk of her Honda and drove back to the Crossroads. She glanced around but didn't see any sign of the bright blue pickup truck. Reassured, she headed inside.

The manager, Tom Poole, greeted her with a friendly smile. "Hi, Kristin, glad to have you."

"Thanks." She shook Tom's hand. "I brought my application and a check for the first month's deposit. Any chance I could move in early?"

"Sure. We normally charge a half-month rate to move in early, but I can waive that in your case. The place is sitting empty anyway."

She relaxed. "Great, thanks."

"Here's more paperwork to sign." Tom slid a lease agreement in front of her, then stepped back to give her time to review the document. It looked pretty straightforward, and she signed off without hesitation.

"Thanks again," she said, handing over the check.

"Oh, I forgot to mention, we offer underground parking, but I don't have a spot available just yet. One should open up in January if you're interested, let me know and I'll reserve it for you. It's an extra fifty bucks a month."

She hesitated, then nodded. "I'd love to park underground, thanks." It was a tad cheaper than what she would have paid for the two-bedroom at her current building, and there the parking was all outside. Keeping her car inside where it was warm, where she didn't have to scrape ice off her windshield throughout the long winter months, was an opportunity she couldn't refuse.

Silently vowing to pick up more shifts to help offset the cost of the move, she took the apartment keys and went to check it out. It was very nice, especially compared to what she was leaving. New appliances, new marble countertops, and freshly painted white walls. There was also the added plus of having laundry facilities in her living space, no sharing in the basement with the rest of the tenants.

She went back to her car to grab the boxes. Precariously stacking them on top of each other, she carried them inside and used her elbow to push the button for the elevator. When the doors opened, she stepped inside and rode up to the fourth floor.

When the doors opened, she couldn't see very well, but she noticed someone standing on the other side. "Excuse me," she said, stepping out.

"Here, let me help." One of the boxes moved out of her line of vision, and she knew she shouldn't have been surprised to see Holt standing there. "Kristin! You're moving in?"

"Yes." Was it possible Holt was on the same floor she was? Really, what were the odds? First Greg and now Holt. "Honestly, this place is cheaper than the others I looked at, plus it's closer to work."

"It's a great place to live," he assured her. "Which apartment?"

"402." She hoped his was on the opposite side of the hallway.

"Mine is 410, so not too far from yours."

Of course it was. With a resigned sigh, she told herself to be grateful his apartment wasn't directly across the hall.

"Here, let me take that." With an ease she envied, Holt took the second box so she could use her key to open the door. He held it open for her so she could go in first.

"Nice." He set both boxes on the counter.

She lifted a brow. "I'm sure it looks just like yours."

He flushed and grinned. "Yeah, it does. Do you have more stuff in your car? I can help you carry everything in."

"Oh, no, I've barely started to pack. I wasn't sure Tom would let me move in early, but he's been super nice about it."

"Tom?" Holt's eyes widened in surprise. "You're on a first-name basis with the manager already?"

"Is that unusual?" She wondered if she insulted him by being so familiar. "I didn't realize."

"No, it's fine. He calls me Dr. Baxter, so I feel compelled to call him Mr. Poole."

"Well, maybe I should do the same." She glanced around, liking the place more and more. "I better head home, I have more packing to do."

"Do you want some help? I don't have any plans for the rest of the day."

"Oh, um, sure." Flustered by his unexpected offer, she couldn't come up with a reason to refuse. "Although you may want to wait until I have some things packed first."

"I don't mind. I'll bring my truck. We can fill it up with

everything that will fit. We can move some of your furniture, too."

"Okay." She blinked, wondering how she'd gone from moving slowly over a couple of weeks to apparently moving over this weekend.

Holt walked with her outside, then gestured to the wide door leading to the underground parking garage. "I'm parked down below. Wait for me, I'll follow you."

"Sure."

He only took two steps before a thin beautiful blonde came rushing over. "Holt? I need to talk to you right away."

It took Kristin a minute to recognize Holt's younger sister, Heidi. In that moment, the magnitude of her mistake hit hard.

Not only would she be constantly running into Holt here at the Crossroads, but she'd likely be seeing Heidi, too.

The nemesis of her past would now be a part of her everyday life.

"Heidi, what's wrong?" Holt tried not to show his impatience, but typical Heidi, arriving without warning and expecting him to drop whatever he was doing for her.

"I need to talk to you." Heidi seemed oblivious to Kristin standing next to the driver's side door of her Honda. He was about to introduce them when Kristin quickly slipped in behind the wheel and started the engine. Before he could blink, she drove away.

With a frustrated sigh, he turned to his sister. "Okay, come on inside."

Heidi was thinner than the last time he'd seen her, which unfortunately reminded him of Barbie, the recent anorexic patient he and Kristin had transported last night. His sister was also pale, her once flawless makeup smudged beneath her eyes as if she'd been crying.

When they reached his apartment, Heidi strode over to look out the window. She sniffled, then turned to face him. "Trent is getting remarried."

He hid a wince. Trent Olson had been the quarterback of the Brookland Bears high school football team. Trent and Heidi had been together since high school, crowned prom king and queen, and had gotten married four years after high school. Trent had graduated from college to become the director of purchasing for Trinity Medical Center, while Heidi had worked in retail selling high-end makeup and hair products. When Heidi had found Trent was cheating on her, she'd crumbled at the abrupt turn her life had taken.

Now her ex-husband was getting remarried.

"I'm sorry, sis." He crossed over to pull Heidi into a hug.

"How could he, Holt? How could he do this to me?"

He bit his tongue, not wanting to point out that since they were divorced and had been for well over a year, Trent had a right to find happiness with someone else.

Something he desperately wished Heidi would do. But instead of moving on, his sister seemed to prefer wallowing in the unfairness of it all.

"I know it's hard, but you need to let him go." Holt felt her stiffen in his arms. "Heidi, holding on to the past is hurting you, not Trent. He's found happiness again, isn't it time for you to do the same?"

"You don't understand." Heidi abruptly pushed away from him, her once beautiful features pulled into a harsh scowl. "He made a laughingstock out of me. Everyone knew he was cheating, except me. Why does he deserve to find happiness again?"

Again, he had to bite his tongue. His sister should be happy that she'd gotten rid of Trent. "When is the wedding?"

"I'm not sure, all I've heard is that it will be soon!" Heidi's green eyes filled with tears. "I bet she's pregnant. That's the only reason I can see for rushing into marriage."

Holt knew that a possible pregnancy was adding salt to an open and festering wound. Heidi had wanted to start a family, but supposedly Trent had wanted to wait until they were financially settled.

If the rumor was true, it was likely the real reason was that he didn't want to have children with Heidi.

"I'm sorry," Holt repeated. "I'm sure it's difficult for you, but like I said, it's time for you to move on with your life. Get out there, start dating again. I'm sure you'll find someone better suited for you than Trent ever was."

"But I l—loved him."

"I know." He glanced at his watch. Every cell in his body wanted to rush Heidi out of there so he could leave to help Kristin. Unfortunately, Kristin was long gone by now, and since he didn't know where she lived, he couldn't head over to help her. "Like I said, sis, you need to let it go."

"I'm so sick and tired of people telling me that." Heidi's gaze burned, but her voice lacked conviction.

He wasn't sure what to say, they'd had this conversation far too many times before. "Have you talked to Mom and Dad lately?"

"No." Heidi sniffed again, but he was glad to see her anger had pushed aside the threat of tears. "Dad thinks I should see a shrink."

He nodded, siding with his dad on this one. "It can't hurt to talk to someone, Heidi. You need to find a way to come to terms with your divorce."

"Whatever." Heidi brushed the idea away as if it were a pesky fly. "I'd hoped you'd understand, but you're just like all the rest."

"Heidi, please don't say that. I care about you, but I don't know what you want me to do about the fact that Trent is getting remarried."

She abruptly brushed past him, heading for the door. "All I ever wanted was your support. Bye, Holt."

He knew she expected him to chase after her, but he didn't. Being with Heidi when she was in one of her moods was exhausting. She claimed she wanted support, but all she really wanted was for everyone around her to validate her feelings of anger and betrayal.

Holt dropped onto his leather sofa with a sigh. He cared about his sister, but rehashing her divorce was not going to change anything. And if he were honest, he'd admit he was annoyed she'd interrupted his Saturday afternoon plans to help Kristin move.

Pathetic to admit he'd far rather help Kristin move than spend time with his sister. Maybe that wasn't entirely fair, Heidi did have the occasional good day where she actually talked about going back to college to finish her degree in marketing.

Something he and their parents strongly encouraged her to do.

His phone rang. His heart quickened with anticipation, but it wasn't Kristin. The call's first three numbers indicated the source was Lifeline. "Hello?"

"Holt? It's Jared O'Connor. Do you have a minute?"

"Of course." No resident would ever refuse to talk to the medical director of the program. "Is something wrong?"

"I'm looking for some resident coverage for the next couple of weeks. You're off on Monday, any chance you could pick up an extra shift? I need coverage for Sunday night into Monday morning."

"Of course, that's no problem." It must be one of the shifts Paulette had been scheduled to work. "Anything you need, Jared."

"Thanks." There was a pause, before Jared added, "Paulette Yost won't be finishing her rotation with us, but I have another potential resident in the wings. I need some time to train her, though."

Her? His gut knotted. "Lana Reasby?"

"Yes. How did you know?" Jared sounded surprised.

He decided to be honest. "She's a friend of Paulette's, and we dated for a while."

"I see. A friend of Paulette's, huh?"

"Yes, sir." He didn't want to ruin anyone's reputation, but he felt compelled to speak his mind. "I'm not sure she'll be much better than Paulette. Lana called me and asked me to put in a good word for Paulette. Claimed Paulette was getting a bad rap from Ivan, although from what I can tell, Ivan's an outstanding paramedic."

"Ivan is, yes." Jared sighed heavily. "Well, that changes things. Maybe I'll just fill in the extra hours myself for the next three months."

"I can work extra, and I'm sure Matt and the other residents would too."

"Thanks, Holt. I appreciate your honesty. Lifeline residents work very closely with the flight staff. More so than they do in the emergency department setting. I don't want to swap one problem for another."

"I agree, and again, we'll make things work. I don't want you to have to pick up all the open shifts."

"I'll hold you to that," Jared said with a chuckle. "Thanks again."

"Jared? Do you know where Kristin Page lives?"

"Why do you ask?" Jared's tone was wary.

Great, now his boss thought he was some sort of creeper. "I offered to help her move and she agreed, but then she had to leave before I could follow her. It's no big deal, I just didn't like the idea of her moving everything on her own."

"Well, I guess I can tell you the building she lives in. It's the older apartment building known as Oak Terrace, located on Oak Drive."

"That works, thanks again." Holt quickly disconnected from the line. He knew where the Oak Terrace apartment building was located, and it was just ten minutes away.

He drove over and parked two spaces down from Kristin's Honda. Peering in through the window of her car, he could see there were a couple of boxes tucked in the back seat.

That meant she'd be out with another box soon, right? All he had to do was to wait.

And hope no one called the police to report him as a suspicious stalker.

As the minutes ticked by slowly, he grew impatient. What if she'd finished packing and wasn't bringing any more boxes out to her car? The sound of voices had him straightening up.

"Kristin, wait."

"Leave me alone, Greg." Kristin was coming toward him with a box in her arms.

Holt came over to meet her, taking the box from her arms. "Need help?"

"Thanks." Her smile was strained, but there was a hint of gratitude in her eyes.

He glanced over her shoulder, recognizing the resident behind her. "Greg Zeman?"

"Oh hey, Holt." Greg's eyes narrowed. "I didn't realize you knew Kristin."

"Leave me alone, Greg." Kristin's tone was weary.

"You should have minded your own business," Greg shot back. "Because of your big mouth, Wendy isn't speaking to me."

"You're the one who decided it was a good idea to introduce us." She unlocked her car and hit the latch of the trunk. "Don't blame me because you didn't like what I had to say."

Greg glared at her, then finally turned away, stalking back inside the apartment complex.

"Sorry about that," Kristin said. "He's the reason I'm moving out."

Suddenly it all made sense. "Former boyfriend."

"Former fiancé," she corrected. "Wendy happens to be another ICU nurse at Trinity. I broke off our engagement after I caught them together."

Ah. So it wasn't just him after all. Kristin's refusal to have dinner had stemmed from how Greg had cheated on her.

Not all men cheated on their wives, fiancées, and girlfriends. His dad was loyal to his mother. And Holt had never cheated on a woman in his life.

Somehow, he needed to find a way to prove to Kristin he would never do that.

But how?

6

Kristin felt better after blurting the truth to Holt about Greg's betrayal. For one thing, it was nice to get the secret off her chest. And secondly, Holt would now know for certain there could be nothing more than friendship between them.

Not that he'd indicated he was deeply attracted to her or anything. An offer to share dinner didn't mean much these days.

She was the one making a bigger deal out of the offer than was necessary.

"Your car is packed to the gills, should we start filling up my truck now?"

Holt's question caught her off guard. "You still want to help?"

"Of course. Why wouldn't I?" He looked confused. "Lots of room in my truck bed for your furniture."

"How do you know? You've never been inside my apartment." She couldn't help feeling exasperated. It was as if Holt was determined to be sweet, nice, and supportive no matter what she said or did.

"You must have a sofa, kitchen table and chairs, right?" He waved at the truck bed. "They should fit in here without a problem."

"Okay, fine. Let's go." Resigned, she led the way back inside. Thankfully, there was no sign of Greg lurking around near her door.

The way Holt had clearly recognized Greg but hadn't asked her anything more about their relationship was interesting. If she didn't know any better, she'd think he was relieved there was nothing more going on with her and Greg.

Nah. Must be her overactive imagination.

Inside her apartment, Holt eyed the sofa. "How strong are you feeling? If you can hold up one end, I can take most of the weight of the sofa as we make it down the stairs. Shouldn't be too difficult."

"Oh yeah? What about getting it up the four flights of stairs at the Crossroads?"

He flashed a grin. "They have a large service elevator. Piece of cake getting it upstairs."

She nodded and flexed her arms. "I lift patients for a living, I'm sure I can manage my end of the sofa."

"Let's do it."

Moving the sofa wasn't as difficult as she'd imagined. Holt took the bulk of the weight on his end, all she needed to do was help guide it. When they had the sofa stored in the back of his truck, they brought down the four kitchen chairs.

"That's it for now, we'll get the table on the second trip," Holt said.

"And my bed and dresser?" She tried not to blush.

"We'll take them, too. The apartment buildings aren't that far apart. It won't take long."

"Okay." Why was she arguing? He was helping her out, saving her the cost of hiring movers or convincing one of her friend's boyfriends to help out.

Holt was easygoing and never seemed to get annoyed with her. Even when she'd changed her mind twice about where to put the sofa.

By the time they finished moving all her stuff, and Holt was kind enough to put her bed frame together for her, it was getting dark outside. "I'll spring for dinner," she announced. "What would you like? Pizza? Chinese? Sandwiches?"

"I could go for Chinese, but you don't need to buy. I'll get it."

"No way. You spent your entire Saturday helping me move, the least I can do is feed you." She picked up her phone and scrolled through her favorite fast-food restaurants. "Anything in particular you don't like or any allergies that I need to know about?"

"Nope. I'm easy." He flashed a grin, and her heart rate jumped up a notch.

"Fine." She forced herself to focus on food, not on what it might be like to kiss Holt. She ordered spicy shrimp, beef and broccoli, sweet and sour chicken, a half dozen egg rolls, and two containers of egg drop soup. When finished, she set her phone aside. "The food will be ready in twenty minutes."

"Sounds good." He stood in her living room. "Place looks better already."

"I really hadn't intended on moving everything on one day." She sighed and dropped into a nearby kitchen chair. "But I have to admit, it's nice to have the hard part finished. The rest of the unpacking shouldn't take long at all."

"Happy to help with the rest, too." Holt didn't look nearly as exhausted as she felt.

"Really, you've done more than enough." She tried to keep her tone firm, secretly worried she'd cave in to the desire of keeping him around longer. "I'm finished moving for tonight. I'll unpack more tomorrow."

"By the way, Jared called and asked me to cover a shift on Sunday night."

"Really?" It took her a moment to understand. "Dr. Frost is out, huh?"

"Frost? That's a good one." Holt grinned, then sobered. "Yeah, Paulette is done at Lifeline, and it sounds like Jared isn't going to replace her."

"Really? I'm surprised. I thought the emergency medicine residents fought for the opportunity to fly with Lifeline."

He hesitated, then nodded. "They do, but the person he had in mind wouldn't be a good fit with the team either."

She thought about the female resident who'd come up to talk to Holt when they'd dropped off their patient with pulmonary hypertension. "Dr. Lana Reasby."

His eyes widened in surprise. "How did you know?"

"I heard what she said to you about ruining Paulette's reputation." She shook her head. "Ridiculous accusation."

A smile tugged at the corner of his mouth. "Thanks. It was ridiculous, and trust me, Lana would not have been any better than Paulette."

"I'm sure." There was no denying her relief over not having to fly with either of the two female residents. Which was, frankly, unusual. Normally the female residents were easier to get along with. Less arrogant than some of the others. Glancing at her watch, she realized it was time to go. "I'll be back in a few minutes."

"Don't be silly, if you're paying, I'm driving." Holt picked up his keys from the counter, then opened the apartment door. "I'm hungry enough to steal a few bites on the way."

She laughed and realized it had been a long time since she'd enjoyed spending time with a man.

With Holt.

Who would have thought her high school crush would turn out to be such a nice guy?

She slid into the passenger seat of Holt's truck, waiting for him to get in behind the wheel. As he drove out of the parking lot, she relaxed against the seat cushion. The fall air turned cool at night, and she knew there were frost warnings out for the following week.

Summer was definitely in the rearview mirror, leaving winter looming up ahead around the curve.

The trip to the closest Chinese restaurant, Ming Lee's, only took them ten minutes. He tried to pay once again, but she stood firm.

They were friends, nothing more.

Inside the truck, the scent of soy sauce and tangy ginger made her mouth water.

Holt glanced at her. "It smells so good I can hardly stand it."

She chuckled and nodded. "I know, but we'll be home soon."

Bright headlights grew closer, the high beams hurting her eyes. She put up her hand to shield them. "Who is that idiot using his brights?"

"I don't know." Holt squinted. "Looks like a small car, maybe the driver can't see very well."

"But in the process he's blinding us." She was irritated with the way some people were rude like that, not caring if their decisions were impacting others.

The lights grew impossibly brighter, almost as if they were coming straight toward them. Her gut clenched, and she braced her hand on the dashboard. "Look out!"

Holt swerved, the wheels along her side of the truck kicking up gravel from the shoulder as he was forced off the road. An instant later, the blur of a red car went flying past them.

The truck ground to a halt, and for long seconds neither of them spoke.

"That was too close." Holt's tone was grim.

"Did you notice the red sports car?" She glanced over at him, trying to read his gaze in the dim interior of the truck. "It looked like the red Corvette Paulette Yost drives."

"I can't believe she would do something like this." His protest came out a little too quick.

"Sure you can. But it's a crazy move on her part. A truck like yours could easily squash her car like a bug."

Holt didn't say anything but put the truck back in gear and pulled back out onto the road.

He might not want to believe the worst, but the way the little red car crossed the center line toward them hadn't been a coincidence.

Not only was Paulette ticked off at Holt, but she wasn't above seeking revenge.

And she didn't seem to care about anyone who happened to stand in her way.

THE RIDE back to Kristin's new apartment didn't take long, but Holt couldn't get her comments about the sporty red car out of his mind.

Had the near collision really been an attempt to cause

them to crash? He couldn't believe a resident would be capable of doing something like that. The physician's Hippocratic Oath was *to do no harm*.

Maybe the car was Paulette's and she just wasn't paying attention. Her being on the highway close to his apartment building could be a coincidence.

He pulled into the underground parking garage and found his assigned space. Kristin didn't say anything as she grabbed the bag of Chinese food and slid out of the passenger seat.

"I'm sorry about that." He rested his hand in the small of her back as they took the elevator up to the fourth floor. "I should have reacted quicker."

She lifted a brow. "I don't see how you could have, it was difficult enough to see anything with the bright lights blinding us."

The idea that Paulette might have tried to hurt them, injuring Kristin in the process, caused his temper to simmer. Even if Paulette hadn't crossed the center line on purpose, she'd been driving recklessly. She should be held responsible for her actions.

"I'll call the police to report the near collision." He took the bag of food and waited while she unlocked her apartment door.

"I was thinking the same thing, but I'm not sure it will do any good." She gestured for him to set the bag on the granite counter. "Did you notice the make and model of the car?"

He slowly shook his head, watching as she pulled plates and silverware out of the cabinets. Kristin wasn't willowy slender, which was one of the things he liked about her. He told himself to stop ogling her like some teenager. "All I saw was a red blob driving past."

She grimaced and set the dishes on the kitchen table. "Me either. A red blur could be anyone."

"Except that Paulette has a reason to resent me." Technically, Ivan was the one who turned her in to Jared, but maybe she'd spoken to Lana and was upset he'd refused to put in a good word for her.

Frankly, it was the only explanation that made sense.

They unpacked the dozens of white cartons of Chinese food, setting them in the center of the table. He took a seat across from Kristin, waiting as she filled her plate first, sampling each of the containers with an enthusiasm he appreciated. No picking at her salad the way Heidi and Lana had done. When she finished, he did the same.

The food was delicious, maybe more so than usual because he was sharing the meal with Kristin. He was deeply grateful to have spent the day with her, even though they'd worked hard moving all her stuff. Everything had been going along great, despite Heidi's interruption, until the near collision on the highway.

He took a bite of his egg roll. "Maybe putting the police on notice is the smart thing to do. That way, if she decides to keep doing crazy stunts, they'd have this issue on file."

Kristin nodded thoughtfully. "I heard rumors about Samantha's ex-husband stalking her earlier in the year, and part of the problem was that she hadn't put the cops on notice right away. Her ex had gone to extremes though, even shooting a gun at the helicopter. I'm sure Paulette won't go that far, but her antics tonight were bad enough."

She was right. That is, if the driver of the red car was really Paulette. Could it have been nothing but a strange coincidence? He stared down at his plate, his appetite vanishing under the heavy weight of concern. "Okay, you've convinced me. I'll call the Brookland police."

Kristin finished her meal and sat back against the chair with a sigh. "That was good."

He couldn't disagree, although he wasn't nearly as hungry as he'd been earlier. When he was finished, he carried his plate to the counter, then pulled out his phone. He had to search for the non-emergency number, then made the call.

Kristin combined cartons of leftovers as he waited for the line to be answered. "Brookland dispatch, how should I direct your call?"

"I'd like to report a reckless driver who nearly caused me to crash less than an hour ago."

"I'll put you through to the officer on duty." There was a brief pause before someone picked up. "Officer Tinsdale."

Holt filled the officer in on what had transpired on the highway. The officer pressed for details, which of course he didn't have. Holt ended the conversation by giving him the information on Paulette Yost. "She's an emergency medicine resident like me and was recently dropped from the Lifeline program. She wanted me to stick up for her, but I refused. She drives a red Corvette, and I just want you to be on notice in case she pulls another stunt."

"I see." Officer Tinsdale tapped the keyboard, then said, "Paulette Yost does have a 1990 red Corvette registered in her name. But you didn't catch the license plate, correct?"

"Correct. Because she had her high beams on." He battled back a wave of frustration. "Again, I just want you to be on notice in case she tries something else."

"Okay, Dr. Baxter, we have your complaint on record. If you see the vehicle again, and can identify it as hers, please let us know."

"I will." He disconnected from the line. "Well, that was useless."

Kristin's smile was wan. "You did the right thing. It's better to have the incident on file, right?"

"Right." He came over to the sink and reached for a drying cloth. She was doing their dishes, so he began to hand dry them. "At least he didn't make me feel like a total idiot."

"You're not an idiot." She lightly brushed his arm, distracting him. "Some people just can't take responsibility for their own actions."

Like the way he hadn't stood up for her nine years ago. He finished drying the dishes, then turned to face her. "Can you forgive me?"

She eyed him warily. "For what?"

He lightly cupped her shoulders in his hands, holding her gaze. "For not telling Heidi to shut up that night in the custard stand."

She averted her gaze. "I thought we settled that? Time to move on, Holt."

He tightened his grip, urging her to look at him. "I need you to forgive me, Kristin. I was young and stupid. I'd gotten so used to blowing off Heidi's snarky comments I didn't really think twice about how you felt. I'm sorry."

Her luminous gaze softened, and she smiled. "Of course I forgive you. It's all in the past."

"Is it? I noticed you took off when Heidi showed up unannounced."

She stiffened, and he instantly regretted bringing the subject up. But wasn't it better to face the past now than to worry about the next time his sister decided to show up without an invitation?

"You're right, I didn't want to talk to Heidi, so I left. It wasn't a big deal, she didn't even recognize me."

"Heidi is too self-absorbed to notice people around her,"

he agreed. "But I want you to know how much I've enjoyed spending the day with you. Sharing Chinese was fun, too."

Kristin's gaze turned wary, but she didn't pull away from him. Instead, he thought he saw a flash of uncertainty in her chameleon green-gray-brown eyes.

Slowly, deliberately, he drew her close, giving her every opportunity to pull away.

She didn't.

The air between them grew thick with tension, and he couldn't seem to tear his gaze from her mouth. He'd never wanted to kiss anyone as badly as he wanted to kiss Kristin.

He bent his head and captured her mouth with his. Heat flared with the intensity of a firecracker when she kissed him back.

7

I f kissing Holt was so wrong, why did it feel so right?

Kristin didn't know how she'd ended up in Holt's arms, but pulling away from his sizzling kiss was the hardest thing she'd ever had to do. She managed, putting a few inches between them, but not pulling away completely.

For a long moment, there was no sound other than their heavy breathing as they gasped for air.

"Do I need to apologize?" Holt's deep voice sent a new wave of shivers down her spine.

"No." The word was little more than a hoarse croak. "But —we can't do this." She forced herself to take another step back, breaking free of his warm embrace. "We work together, remember? And I don't date doctors."

The corner of his mouth kicked up in a lopsided smile. "We only work together for a few months, and maybe you should rephrase that last statement. You don't date doctors who cheat. Something I'd never do."

The way he said those words, looking deep into her eyes, made her want to believe him. But truly what man went into a relationship thinking, *oh yeah, if I get tired of her, I'll just find someone else.*

Cheating wasn't something that people planned for. It just happened.

Didn't it?

She gave herself a mental shake. It didn't matter because she had no intention of dating Holt Baxter.

"It's late, and I'm exhausted." She forced a smile. "Good night, Holt."

"Good night, Kristin." He looked as if he might kiss her again, but she went around him toward the apartment door. He smiled as if reading her mind. "Let me know if you need any more help tomorrow."

"I'll be fine, but thanks. I appreciate everything you did for me."

He nodded and disappeared down the hall to his apartment. A walk that took all of fifteen steps. She closed the door, shot the deadbolt home, and leaned weakly against the frame, wondering just what she'd gotten herself into.

Staying away from Holt who lived just down the hall would not be easy. Especially after that kiss.

She closed her eyes, reliving the moment. Holt's kiss had been incredible, not just because she'd always been attracted to him, starting back when she was seventeen to his eighteen, but because he'd kissed her as if he'd cherished her. With a mixture of wanton need and sweetness that was oh-so-tempting.

Nothing even close to the way Greg used to kiss. As if he saw kissing her as a means to an end.

Enough. She pushed away from the door and abolished thoughts of Greg Zeman from her mind. She put the leftovers away in the fridge, then headed to bed.

Being physically exhausted helped her sleep, and the following day she decided to finish unpacking the boxes Holt had helped her move. Normally she liked working alone, listening to music as she unpacked, but her thoughts kept straying to Holt.

His adorable smile. His husky laugh. His passionate kiss.

When her phone rang, she almost dropped the glass bowl on her tiled kitchen floor. Setting it on the counter, she reached for her phone, recognizing the number as coming from Lifeline.

"Hello?"

"Hey, Kristin, it's Jared. Ivan called off work tonight, I was hoping you'd be able to cover for him."

"Sure, that's fine. I hope Ivan is okay?"

There was a slight hesitation before Jared responded, "Me, too. He didn't say much, so I'm not sure if the issue is with him or his daughter. Either way, I'm glad you can cover. Thanks a lot."

Jared quickly disengaged from the call. She set her phone aside, thinking about whether or not she should try to take a nap before going in, when she remembered Holt was also working tonight.

If she didn't know better, she'd think God was pushing them together on purpose.

Her attempt to sleep a couple of hours was a dismal failure. A cold shower helped wake her up, and as she headed out the door of her apartment, she ran smack into Holt.

"Oh, hey." She hoped he didn't notice how flustered she was. "I'm heading to work, too." As if he wouldn't figure that out while she was wearing the same one-piece navy flight suit he wore.

"I know, I heard you agreed to cover Ivan's shift. Figured I'd give you a ride. No reason for both of us to drive."

Carpooling for a ten-minute trip? She suppressed a sigh, knowing it would be petty to refuse. "Sounds good."

There was no sign of the red Corvette this trip, and as Holt drove past the spot where they'd gone off the road, she could see deep tire tracks in the gravel.

"This will be my first night shift." Holt's voice cut into her thoughts. "Hope I can stay awake."

"We'll keep each other awake." His smile widened, and she flushed when she realized how that might sound. She hastened to add, "I play a mean game of cribbage."

"Never played. You'll have to teach me."

"It's not difficult, but we can play gin rummy, too." She hoped they would get enough calls that they wouldn't be forced to chat all night. There wasn't enough small talk in the world to fill thirteen hours.

"I wouldn't mind learning cribbage." Holt pulled into the parking lot, choosing a space close to the building.

"Great." As they walked into the hangar together, it occurred to her how others might think they'd spent the day together.

And the night.

Ugh. The last thing she wanted was to be the subject of the Lifeline rumor mill. When they entered the debriefing room, Reese was there, along with the new pilot, a woman named Megan Hoffman. Kristin had flown with her a couple of times and was impressed by her ability.

"Hi, Kristin, Holt." Reese nodded at them. "Thanks for coming in."

"I hope Ivan is okay," Jenna said with a frown. "It's not like him to call off, other than for his daughter."

"I know." Kristin liked Jenna Reed, too. She was a great paramedic and engaged to one of their former residents, Zane Taylor. Their wedding was scheduled for April of next year. Jenna was also going back to school to pursue her nursing degree, attending college at the same university as her younger sister, Rae. Kristin gave Jenna credit, it wasn't easy to work full time, attend classes, and plan a wedding.

Overall, Kristin liked everyone she worked with, it was the residents who rotated in and out that added a very different dimension. Like Holt. And Paulette. "Hopefully Ivan will be back soon."

"There's a transfer pending from the Great Lakes naval base, near the Illinois border," Jenna informed them. She'd been paired to fly with resident Matt Abbot. "The guy took a turn for the worse, so the transfer is on hold, but I suspect they'll call back soon."

"What happened?" Holt asked. "Why would we get a transfer from the naval base?"

"Sounded as if one of their new recruits got super sick and is now intubated on a vent, with signs of multisystem organ failure." Matt shrugged. "They don't have a good explanation for what happened, other than possibly an autoimmune reaction to receiving the vaccinations."

"That doesn't seem right," Holt protested.

Matt spread his hands. "Hey, I'm just passing along the information we received. Could be they have completely different information by now."

"Maybe." Holt didn't look satisfied. "Anything else?"

"Nope. Overall a good day." Matt stood. "Hope you don't get too many calls."

Secretly, Kristin hoped they did.

～

HOLT WAS SEATED opposite from Kristin with the cribbage

board between them when their pagers went off. She'd just started explaining the intricacies of the game, which were difficult to concentrate on with her cinnamon scent teasing his senses.

"Great Lakes naval base," she said, reading their text page. She met his gaze. "Guess this means our guy's condition has stabilized."

"Let's go." Holt couldn't deny that he was interested to find out more about their young recruit.

As they settled in the chopper with Megan Hoffman behind the stick, he listened as she spoke to the paramedic base. "Estimated flight time thirty minutes."

This would be his longest flight so far, and it was only his third shift.

All of which he'd been fortunate enough to have Kristin as his partner.

Flying at night was strange. There was nothing but inky blackness out the windows. He knew their job was to help watch for birds, the biggest threat to a chopper was being knocked off course by a bird strike, but darned if he could see much of anything out there.

"Nervous?"

He glanced at Kristin. There were low interior lights in the hull of the helicopter, but it was difficult to read her expression through her face mask. "Not really. Should I be?"

There was a slight hesitation before she responded, "No, of course not. Megan is an awesome pilot; she can handle night flying just fine."

In other words, flying at night was more dangerous than flying during the day. Okay, then. Good to know. However, since there was nothing he could do about that, he shrugged it off and tried to focus on their patient.

He cued his mic. "Megan, when we're ten minutes from our destination, I'd like to speak to the physician on duty to get an update on our patient."

"Ten-four, Dr. Baxter."

"Please, call me Holt." Working with a small team like Lifeline's, there was no reason to be so formal.

As promised, Megan communicated through the paramedic base to reach the doctor on call within the Great Lakes naval base. "Dr. Richter is on the line for you, Dr. Baxter."

"Thanks." Holt cleared his throat. "Dr. Richter, I'd like a report on our patient's condition."

"Jason Hicks is a nineteen-year-old new recruit who fell ill two days ago after receiving a multitude of immunizations, which all of our new recruits receive, normally without a problem. Unfortunately, Jason's condition continued to deteriorate until we were forced to intubate him and initiate vasopressors to stabilize him."

He glanced at Kristin who was listening in. The poor kid's condition didn't sound good. "What vasopressors?"

"Norepinephrine and vasopressin. He's not maxed out on either of them, yet."

Yet? "So you've been titrating them up?"

"Yes. But not as aggressively as yesterday."

That wasn't saying much. "I understand he's in multisystem organ failure."

"His labs are getting better, but his kidneys have taken a hit. We have him on continuous renal replacement therapy."

Kristin gave a slight shake of her head, indicating they couldn't provide that service in-flight.

"Anything else? I can't believe all of this is an autoimmune response to his immunizations."

"We don't have any other explanation at this point," Dr. Richter said. "I'd be interested if the team at Trinity Medical Center find otherwise."

"Understood, thanks. We should be there in less than ten minutes."

Holt clicked off the mic and drew in a deep breath. The kid's condition might be somewhat stable, but this would still be a tenuous flight. One he was grateful to be making with Kristin at his side.

Megan dropped the bird on the rooftop landing pad. He and Kristin didn't have to talk, they knew what needed to be done. Inside the Great Lakes Medical Hospital, the ICU was located on the second floor.

Dr. Richter was a young man, just a few years older than Holt from what he could tell. Richter was dressed in a uniform instead of scrubs, his hair cut military short, and he sported Captain bars on his sleeves.

Jason Hicks looked younger than his nineteen years, surrounded by more equipment than Holt had ever seen. The renal replacement therapy machine looked a bit like a dialysis machine, with a giant filter and four large bags of fluid suspended on various poles. Kristin and the ICU nurse discussed their strategy of how to swap over the equipment, while Richter pulled up the young man's chart on a large computer screen.

"Here are his latest labs, hot off the press." Richter gestured to the screen. "You can see the CRRT is helping to correct his underlying acidosis."

"That's good, but we don't have the ability to keep that going during the flight. Have you ruled out all sources of possible sepsis?"

"So far every blood culture has come back negative. We

did start him on broad-spectrum antibiotics just to be on the safe side."

Holt stared at the screen, trying to figure out if he was missing anything. "Okay, anything else you think I should know?"

Richter shook his head. "I wish I had more information for you."

"Family?"

"We called his mother. She'll be heading up to Trinity Medical Center, tonight yet." Richter held out his hand. "I'm sure he'll do fine. Those specialists at Trinity Medical Center are experts. They'll figure out what's going on."

"I'm sure they will." Holt felt good about the reputation of the hospital he was training in. He crossed over to Kristin. "Ready to get him onto the gurney?"

Within five minutes, they had Jason Hicks bundled on their gurney and were taking him up to the helicopter. Megan was waiting patiently, and soon they were in the air, heading back toward Milwaukee.

Kristin put the headphones over Jason's ears, even though the guy was sedated. He wasn't about to question her methods, he'd learned from the flight with Barbie, their anorexic patient, to anticipate the unexpected.

The first few minutes of the flight passed by without issue. But all too soon, Jason's heart began having arrhythmias.

"Give a bolus of amiodarone." Even as he gave the order, he knew that the electrolyte imbalance might be the culprit.

Unfortunately, they couldn't do any lab testing hundreds of miles in the air.

After the bolus was in, Kristin looked at him. "Which way was his potassium trending prior to being started on CRRT?"

He thought back to the data on the screen. "He'd been trending high, a result of his kidney failure."

"We could consider giving a bolus of insulin and D50, see if that helps."

"Good idea, let's do it." Again, he appreciated her subtle cues.

Once those infusions were in, they both watched the heart rate on the screen. The premature ventricular beats became fewer and farther apart.

But suddenly, Jason began to cough with such force that the endotracheal tube came flying out. Holt looked at it with horror, then moved so he was positioned behind Jason's head.

"Get me another size seven tube and the laryngoscope." He drew gloves over his damp palms as he realized the breathing tube had to be replaced ASAP.

"Here." Kristin deftly opened the tube, then handed him the laryngoscope. "Would you like me to increase his sedation?"

"Yes." He focused on getting the breathing tube back into Jason's trachea. Unfortunately, the poor kid's throat was inflamed and swollen, making it almost impossible to visualize the vocal cords.

"Pulse ox eighty percent," Kristin said.

No! He couldn't lose this kid.

Sweat ran down the sides of his face beneath the helmet. He tried again, silently praying that he had the skill to replace this breathing tube.

He blindly inserted the tube and reached for the small device they used to check for placement. The color metric device on the end turned yellow, indicating he was in the right spot.

After quickly connecting the ventilator tubing, he held the tube firmly in place so Kristin could fasten it in place.

"Thank goodness," he murmured.

"Pulse ox is still hanging around eighty-two percent."

"What FIO2 is he on?"

"Fifty percent."

"Turn it up to sixty percent."

Sweat continued to roll down his face as the kid's pulse ox refused to budge. He tried not to panic. "Maybe we should go up a little more to sixty-five percent. Just until he recovers."

Kristin obliged, but still, Jason's pulse ox remained about 85%.

Holt stared at the young man, trying to figure out what he was missing. Then he saw the way the right side of his chest looked puffy compared to the left side. "Hand me an eighteen- gauge needle. I think he has a spontaneous pneumothorax."

"From losing the ETT?" Kristin opened the needle for him, then moved the kid's gown to scrub his chest.

For the second time in a handful of days, he inserted the needle into the space between the fourth and fifth intercostal space.

Within seconds, Jason's pulse ox improved to 92%. But then his heart rate went into full-blown ventricular tachycardia.

A life-threatening heart rhythm. They were going to lose him!

"Get the defib." He pulled the kid's gown all the way off so Kristin could place the patch on his chest, then turned him to put one on his back. She dialed up the defib.

"All clear?"

She shocked him once. Then twice, then a third time.

Jason's heart converted into a normal sinus rhythm, but for how long?

"Megan, what's our ETA?"

"Fifteen minutes."

Holt tried not to wince. Fifteen minutes to keep this kid alive. No easy task. He resorted to praying again.

Losing this patient en route was not an option.

8

Kristin stared down at the young navy recruit whose life hung by a whisper of thread. Nineteen was too young to die, especially when it was clear the providers didn't know what exactly was wrong with him.

A car crash or some other type of trauma was one thing. A mystery disease causing multisystem organ failure was completely different.

Tension radiated off Holt, and she knew he was concerned about what might happen if the Lifeline team lost another patient. Even the most highly skilled doctors and nurses couldn't save everyone, but if this young man died, she knew Holt would take it personally.

"Pulse ox stable at ninety-four percent, pulse one ten, and BP ninety-two over fifty-eight." She rattled off Jason's vital signs, mostly to help Holt relax a bit.

"Give a bolus of amiodarone." Holt's expression was grim. "I want to be sure we support his heart as much as possible."

She nodded and began preparing the medication. A

couple of premature ventricular beats skipped across the small EKG monitor. Her stomach knotted. Suffering a spontaneous pneumothorax could have been the cause of Jason's V-tach, but seeing the ongoing irritability in his heart rhythm, she was concerned there was something more going on.

"Amiodarone infusing now." Her gaze went between the medication infusing into Jason's IV and the heart monitor. The premature beats continued, not frequently enough to require a shock, but more than she liked.

"I'm concerned he has cardiomyopathy from whatever is going on with his immune system." Holt's green gaze caught hers. "I need to talk to the cardiology team at Trinity."

She nodded and listened as he spoke to the paramedic base. Within two minutes, Holt was connected to the cardiology fellow on call at Trinity Medical Center.

"You should be prepared to place this kid on an intra-aortic balloon pump," Holt was saying. "He's already gone into V-tach once, which we were able to convert, but he's still showing signs of heart damage."

"Understood, I'll call the cardiac perfusionist in and have the IABP on standby for when you arrive. Thanks for the heads-up."

"No problem. See you soon." Holt disconnected from the call, and she sensed his tension easing a bit.

"ETA eight minutes," Megan informed them.

More premature beats fluttered across the screen. His blood pressure dipped a bit farther, and she found herself holding her breath.

Come on, Jason, she silently urged. *Hang in there for just a little while longer.*

"When the amiodarone bolus is finished, start continuous infusion," Holt said.

"What dose and rate?" She prepared the infusion even though the bolus should run for fifteen minutes. She didn't want it to run out while they were unloading him from the back of the chopper.

Holt gave her the medication parameters, and when she finished with the IV bag, she quickly programmed the IV pump to run at the ordered rate. When the infusion was ready to go, she connected it to the second port of his central line, keeping the pump on standby so there would be no delay once the bolus was finished.

The next eight minutes seemed to pass in slow motion. Finally, Megan banked the bird and began to descend, letting them know they'd be landing at Trinity shortly.

Their decent seemed to take forever. Once they landed, Holt jumped out and ran to the back of the helicopter to open the hatch. She eyed the bolus, taking note that there was still almost three minutes of infusion time left. After pushing the gurney toward Holt, she jumped down and hurried over to assist.

There was no way to talk over the noise of the whirling blades, but her gaze met Holt's briefly, and a moment of shared understanding passed between them. They ran, pushing the gurney into the building and hitting the elevator button.

Inside the elevator, she stripped off her helmet and stashed it beneath the gurney. Holt did the same, between providing breaths with the Ambu bag. As they rode down to the fourth floor cardiac intensive care unit, the amiodarone bolus finished.

The elevator doors opened. "Hold on." She quickly shut down the IV pump with the bolus and started up the second IV pump with the continuous infusion.

Holt held the elevator door open, waiting for her to

finish. As they began wheeling the gurney out into the hall, their portable heart monitor began to alarm.

"He's in V-tach again." Holt's voice was hoarse with fear.

"The defib is still connected." Keeping calm in an emergency was critical in these situations, but she had to admit that having a patient cardiac arrest in the hallway was a first. "I'm charging it up, all clear?" She pushed the defib button. Jason's heart rhythm didn't convert. "Charging again, all clear?" She waited for Holt to finish giving a breath, then hit the defib button.

This time it worked. Jason's heart converted to a normal rhythm. "Hurry," Holt urged. "It's only a matter of time until he codes again."

She knew he was right. This young man needed far more support than the two of them could provide. They rushed the gurney down the hall and pushed through the wide double doors of the cardiac ICU.

As promised, the cardiology fellow was waiting for them. As they pushed the gurney into the open room, the heart monitor began to triple beep yet again.

"We gave two shocks in the hallway on the way in," Holt said as she charged up the defib again. "He's been given a bolus of amiodarone and is on a drip."

"We'll need to increase the rate," the fellow said.

"Defib is charged, all clear?" Kristin repeated the same sequence of events, this time giving three shocks before Jason's heart rhythm stabilized.

A team of nurses came over to assist, and it didn't take long to get Jason switched over to the ICU equipment. As she stepped back, she watched as the cardiology fellow began to prep Jason's groin for a large-bore central line, needed to access his heart so they could insert the intra-aortic balloon pump.

Holt joined her near the foot of Jason's bedside. They stayed out of the way of the care team, but close enough to see what was happening. She knew they should leave, but she couldn't make her feet move. The increased dose of amiodarone appeared to be helping, but the ICU team ended up shocking him two more times before they had the intra-aortic balloon pump up and running.

Once Jason's heart had been given the extra support it needed, the young man's heart rate settled down to ninety beats per minute, with less premature ventricular beats fluttering across the screen.

So far, he was holding his own. They'd gotten him here just in time.

She glanced at Holt. "Megan's waiting."

"I know." He looked worn out yet relieved as they turned away.

Thankfully, Megan didn't seem fazed by their tardiness. Maybe because she'd known how tenuous their patient's condition had been and allowed them extra time to perform the hand-off. The trip back to the Lifeline hangar was quick. Holt disappeared into the lounge, but she carried their duffel bag over to the supply room to restock.

When she'd finished, she headed into the lounge. Holt sat with his head cradled in his hands as if the weight of the world was on his shoulders.

"Hey, we did a good job up there." She dropped onto the sofa beside him.

"Yeah." His voice was muffled. She heard him draw in a harsh breath. He scrubbed his hands over his face, then sat up to look at her. "I should have increased his amiodarone infusion. I don't know why I didn't think of that."

Really? That's what this self-recrimination was about? "Holt, things were happening very fast. And when would you have increased the drip? After the second code in the middle of the hallway? At that point the best option was to get him into the ICU as quickly as possible."

His vulnerable green gaze clung to hers. "You think so?"

"Yes." She lightly squeezed his forearm. "We did good, Holt. That kid is super sick, but with our help, he's now at Trinity getting the best care possible."

He nodded and rubbed the center of his chest with a rueful smile. "I thought I might go into V-tach when he coded in the hallway like that."

She let out a husky laugh. "I know what you mean. That was the first time I've ever shocked a patient in the middle of the hallway."

He slid an arm around her shoulders in a brief hug. "I'm glad you were there. You're the best flight partner a guy could ask for."

"Ditto." She flushed at the compliment. His musky clean scent made her long to lean against him, nestling her head in the hollow of his shoulder. Memories of their hot kiss made her pulse jump. How was it possible that her attraction to this man hadn't dimmed over the course of nearly a decade?

It was abnormal. She was abnormal.

"Kristin?" Megan's voice had her jumping away from Holt as if they'd been caught kissing rather than being in a casual embrace.

"What do you need?" She walked toward their pilot, putting badly needed distance between them.

Megan eyed her curiously but didn't say anything. "I just wanted to let you know the wind is kicking up. They're at about thirty miles per hour now, but if the gusts continue as predicted, they could reach forty-five miles per hour. We can't fly in those conditions."

Knowing high winds were just as much of a threat as snow and ice, she nodded. "Okay, thanks for letting us know."

"I'll keep you posted." With another curious glance between her and Holt, Megan returned to the debriefing room where there was a live satellite view of the weather conditions up at all times.

She turned to face Holt. "Sounds like we may be grounded."

He yawned and nodded. "I heard. Guess it's time for you to teach me to play cribbage again."

"Why not?" She fetched the cribbage board and deck of cards out of the cupboard over the coffeemaker.

Being grounded with Holt for the next nine hours would wreak havoc on her emotions.

She was beginning to care about him, far more than she should. Yet regardless of how nice of a guy Holt seemed to be, there was no way on this green earth she was going to trust him with her heart.

AFTER THE EMOTIONALLY DRAINING START OF his shift, Holt was surprised the rest of the night proved uneventful.

"You win, again!" He tossed his cards down with a disgusted sigh. "Whatever happened to beginner's luck?"

"Don't worry, you'll get better." Her patronizing tone made him smile.

"Enough." Kristin pushed away from the table. "I need to move around. I think we should do a couple of transport follow-up visits."

"Are you sure it's okay to leave the hangar?" It wasn't so much that he didn't trust her, but surely leaving the area where the helicopter was located went against the rules. "Megan said the winds have died down a bit. I know it's at the end of our shift, but we could still get a call."

"We have pagers and the hospital isn't far." She rose and stretched. "But if you'd rather stay here, that's fine with me. Follow-up visits don't take two people."

"I'd rather go with you. I haven't done any follow-ups yet." Over the past several hours, he'd sensed Kristin trying to pull away from him, at least on a personal level. Every time he tried to talk about the past, she asked detailed medical questions about patients she'd taken care of in the past or presenting hypothetical scenarios for the future.

If he didn't know better, he'd think she was studying for her MCATs, the exam required to get into medical school.

"Okay, let's go. I'll let Megan know in case she needs us."

He waited for Kristin to pop her head into the debriefing room to let Megan know their plans. After they donned navy blue Lifeline jackets, she picked up an electronic tablet before heading outside.

The wind held a definite chill, indicating winter was indeed right around the corner. He followed Kristin as she briskly walked toward Trinity Medical Center. One thing was for sure, the cold air helped wake him up. He'd stopped drinking coffee at roughly two in the morning and was feeling the impact of running on no sleep for twenty-four hours.

Inside the warmth of the building, Kristin paused and glanced down at her tablet. "I thought we'd check on our patients first, before we do the others."

"Fine with me." Who was he to argue?

"Let's head to the neuro intensive care unit first. Leo Campine is still a patient up there."

"Leo Campine?" He thought for a moment. "Oh, I remember. Motorcycle crash."

"Yes." She led the way to the elevators that would take them to the fifth floor.

Despite the early hour, there was a bustle of activity wherever they went. Hospitals didn't sleep, especially not in the critical care areas.

They found Leo without difficulty, and he stood by as Kristin spoke with the nurse.

"His neuro status is improving; we're in the process of weaning him off the vent."

"That's good news." Kristin entered a note on the screen. "I'm glad to hear he's doing better."

Holt gazed at their patient, realizing he and Kristin had played an important role in his care. Feeling better, he gamely followed her to the cardiac ICU.

It was early to be checking in on Jason's condition, but he was glad she'd decided to stop there next. Honestly, the kid didn't look much better, although his vitals were stable. The cardiology fellow was still at the bedside, along with two nurses, and Holt knew they'd been keeping a close eye on him for the past few hours.

The fellow looked over at him in surprise. "Hey, what's up?"

"Just checking in." He gestured to the pale figure lying amidst the tubes and lines. "Any update on what might be going on?"

"Not really. We have a slew of labs pending, but right now the plan is to continue treating his symptoms. He's gone into renal failure, so we're doing continuous dialysis on him. We have several consults pending, so we may know more in a day or two."

"Sounds good." He nodded and stepped back. It was

reassuring to know Jason was still alive, even if he wasn't nearly out of the woods yet.

"Next up, Barbie Martin." Kristin glanced at him. "She's still in the medical ICU."

He remembered the anorexic girl who'd pulled out her central line during their flight. Next to Jason, she'd been one of the most difficult transports he'd participated in.

As they walked into the unit, he could hear the sound of muffled sobs. Not necessarily unusual in a critical care area, where the sickest of the sick were taken care of.

Kristin stood in front of the census board, then glanced back at him. "She's in room ten."

As they closed in on room ten, the sounds of crying increased. Kristin hesitated outside the doorway, glancing up at the multiple heart rhythm strips displayed on the monitor overhead, then took a hasty step back.

"What is it?" he whispered so the two people hugging and crying in the room couldn't hear.

"I—she's gone." Kristin's face was pale. As they tried to ease away, the sobbing woman noticed them.

"Oh, it's you." Barbie's mother swiped at her eyes and broke away from her husband's embrace. "I'm glad you're here. I wanted to thank you."

Kristin stepped forward, her expression full of compassion. "There's no need to thank us. I'm so sorry for your loss."

Barbie's mother's eyes filled with more tears. "I just don't understand why she couldn't get past her anxiety around eating food. It just doesn't make sense. I know the kids used to tease her about being overweight, but that was when she was fourteen." Barbie's mother glanced over her shoulder at the painfully thin daughter lying unmoving on the bed. "If only she could have gotten over her fears . . ."

Holt frowned, trying to follow the woman's line of thought. Was she saying that Barbie's illness had started because she'd been teased over being fat? That thoughtless cruel comments had caused this poor girl to go down a path of literally starving herself to death?

"I know it's not easy to understand what goes on in a teenager's mind. Please know we are so sorry for your loss."

"Thank you."

Kristin gave Barbie's mother a hug, and when she turned away, he could see tears shimmering in her green/gray/brown eyes.

The wounded expression in her eyes hit him in the gut like a sucker punch. He understood better now just how much Heidi's comments must have hurt Kristin all those years ago.

And how strong Kristin was to have overcome her past to become the amazing nurse she was now.

9

After doing her best to comfort Barbie's mother, Kristin wanted nothing more than to head back to the hangar.

This was part of the problem with follow-up visits. Sometimes you discovered patients didn't make it.

A twenty-year-old had died for no good reason. Oh, she knew that the mean girls who'd once called Barbie fat weren't responsible for her death, but they absolutely had sent a young girl down a dangerous path.

Pushing blindly past Holt, she left the ICU. Blinking away her tears, she decided they should take the stairs down to the lobby level. Without saying anything to Holt, she entered the stairwell and went down.

He kept pace behind her. She sensed he wanted to talk, but she didn't.

All she wanted to do was head home. Unfortunately, she'd agreed to ride to work with Holt, which meant she'd have to endure his company for a while longer.

When they returned to the hangar, she filed the follow-up reports she'd performed in Jared's mailbox. The fact that

Barbie Martin had died wouldn't impact their statistics, but the young girl's passing haunted her just the same. When she returned to the debriefing room, resident Matt Abbott had arrived. He glanced at her and Holt. "Hey, how was your night?"

"Started off with a shaky transfer, but after that, nothing," Holt answered when Kristin didn't. "The wind kicked up overnight, so we were grounded for a while."

"Bummer." Matt looked dejected. "Twelve-hour shifts are long when you don't get many calls."

Tell me about it, she thought. But she didn't say anything, just took a seat next to Matt and waited for Kate to arrive.

Nate was the day shift pilot. He and Megan crowded around the satellite image, discussing the weather conditions. When Kate showed up, Kristin filled them both in on the details of their tenuous transfer.

"He coded in the hallway?" Kate echoed. "That's terrible."

"Moral of that story is that I should have increased the amiodarone infusion," Holt said, addressing Matt. "Kid is hanging in there, though. We did a quick follow-up visit this morning."

"Interesting case," Matt agreed.

Kristin yawned and glanced at her watch. "I'm exhausted."

"Me, too." Holt picked up on cue. "Hope you guys have a good shift."

She followed Holt out of the debriefing room, feeling self-conscious that they'd be walking to the same car together, and driving home together. She needed to switch a few shifts with Kate, who seemed paired up with Matt. Kate was happily married to a former emergency medicine resident, Ethan Weber. Despite her experience with Greg, there were a few Lifeline staff members who'd ended up married or engaged to physicians.

But she had no intention of following in their footsteps.

Always the gentleman, Holt opened her car door for her. She slid into the passenger seat, shivering in the cool temperatures. When Holt took his seat behind the wheel, he turned on the engine and gestured to the controls. "Heated seats, if you're interested."

"Really?" It was a luxury she didn't have in her car. Leaning forward, she pushed the button for her side and within seconds felt the warmth of the seat seep into her bones. "Nice."

Holt flashed a smile as he drove out of the parking lot. "Do you mind if I ask you a question?"

She tensed. "Maybe, depends on what it is."

He hesitated. "I'd like to know how you became to be such a confident, talented nurse. I mean, look at what happened to Barbie?"

Not this again. She wished Holt would stop going back to rehash the past. Especially since being compared to an anorexic patient wasn't very complimentary. Yet, it was obvious he was struggling with how his sister had treated her, and she understood his concern.

"We can't pass judgment on what Barbie went through. Her mother only knows what her daughter said, but it could be that Barbie experienced a higher level of bullying than I did."

Holt opened his mouth as if to protest, but then caught himself. "I'm more interested in how you coped."

She shrugged, glad the trip to the Crossroads wouldn't take long. "College helped. Every freshman had the same lowly position on campus, and suddenly the popular pretty girls weren't anything special. There were dozens of others just like them. It made me realize that high school wasn't the real world. In many respects, brains mattered more in college than in high school. And thankfully, I was smart enough to get into the nursing program ahead of some of the former pretty, popular girls."

Holt nodded thoughtfully. "I agree. I remember thinking the same thing in college. Who we were in high school was nothing compared to where we were headed."

"Exactly." She was surprised he seemed to understand what she was talking about. A guy who looked like Holt— tall, dark, broad shoulders, and handsome with to-die-for-green eyes—should have had a seamless transition into college life.

He pulled into the underground parking garage and parked in the same spot he'd had before. The spaces were clearly assigned to each apartment, but there must be more apartments than parking spaces available.

"Thanks again for the ride." She climbed out of the truck without waiting for him to open her door. The more time she spent with Holt the more it felt as if they were becoming more than friends. This *closeness* had to stop.

But, of course, Holt walked with her to the elevator and up to the fourth floor. She'd expected him to veer off toward his own unit, but he followed her all the way to her door.

"Sleep well, I'll see you later." She smiled up at him, then quickly unlocked the door and went inside.

"Good night, Kristin." His words wafted toward her, soft and husky, moments before she closed the door. For a moment she leaned weakly against the door, then pushed herself upright.

She really needed to get over him. Her innate response to him.

Her attraction to him.

Despite being up more than twenty-four hours, she didn't sleep well. Working the night shift had never agreed with her. Her brain was hardwired to be active during the day and shut down at night, not the other way around.

After barely four hours of sleep, she dragged herself up and padded bleary-eyed into the kitchen. She filled the coffee carafe with water, then poured it into the top of her coffeemaker without remembering to open the lid.

Water splashed all over the counter, on her pajamas, and ran in rivulets onto the floor. With a sigh, she mopped up the mess and tried again, this time managing to complete the task of making a pot of coffee.

A cup of coffee and a shower helped her feel human, but her head still ached from lack of sleep, and she had the energy of a sloth. After watching several movies on Netflix, she'd had enough of sitting around. It was time to get out of the apartment, even for a short while.

She wasn't a regular runner, more of a once or twice a week kind of thing, but today she decided exercising in the fresh air would be a good way to clear the cobwebs from her brain.

Dressed in her running gear, she peeked out of her apartment door, half expecting to see Holt standing in the hallway waiting for her. Finding the hallway empty, she let out a soundless sigh of relief and left the apartment, locking the door behind her.

She took the stairs down to the main level. Outside, the sun shone brightly on the green, yellow, and orange leaves of the trees. Autumn in Wisconsin was beautiful. As much as she hated their long winters, she enjoyed living in an area with changing seasons.

Her running form was nothing fancy, she didn't have a lithe athletic figure by any means. She enjoyed food too much to skip meals and couldn't fathom starving herself the way Barbie had done. But exercise was part of maintaining a healthy lifestyle, so she was determined to at least attempt to stay in some sort of shape. Running was one way to do that, not that she planned to break any speed or distance records.

The first few yards always seemed the hardest, but soon she fell into a decent rhythm. She rounded the apartment complex and headed out toward the park located a half mile down the road.

There were a couple of teenage boys with gloves playing catch and a few women strolling through the park. She didn't really pay much attention, too busy concentrating on breathing slow and easy.

When she estimated she'd gone about a mile and a half —again, no long-distance running for her—she turned around to head back.

She kept her gaze on the apartment building up ahead. After passing by the park, something hard slammed her in the center of her back, knocking her off balance. She tumbled forward, hitting the pavement hard with her hands and knees. Somehow, she broke her fall enough to roll sideways, preventing herself from face-planting on the asphalt.

Sprawled on the ground, she was so stunned she couldn't think. What had happened? She saw the baseball lying in the grass several feet away.

No way. The kids had hit her? On purpose?

She struggled to her feet, wincing at the various aches and pains shooting through her body. Her hands and knees had taken the brunt of her fall, but her shoulder and back throbbed, too. She was grateful she hadn't hit her head.

Sweeping her gaze over the park, she tried to find the

kids who'd been playing catch. But they weren't anywhere in sight. The women had vanished, too.

Limping badly, her right knee was beginning to swell. She went over to pick up the baseball. She tossed it lightly in the air, catching it in her palm. She hadn't imagined the event, and the baseball was proof. The kids must have thought it would be funny to hit a runner, then had taken off once she'd fallen to the ground.

Still, she thought it was odd. The kids hadn't seemed to notice her running by. They were calling out to each other, tossing the ball high in the air, hooting and hollering as if practicing catching a fly ball. She figured they were on some sort of school baseball team.

Had their aim been off that badly? She stared at the ball, then back over the park. Where were the women who'd been there?

The sudden emptiness of the park made her shiver.

Kristin told herself to stop seeing something sinister in what clearly had been meant to be a prank. The kids must have thrown it harder than they'd intended.

Running the rest of the way back to her apartment was out of the question, so she walked. Or rather limped. She carried the ball, as if needing tangible evidence that she hadn't tripped over her own two feet like some sort of imbecile.

Preoccupied with thoughts of soaking her sore muscles in a hot tub, she didn't see Holt until she nearly ran into him coming off the elevator.

"Excuse me." She winced when her knee protested the abrupt stop.

"What's wrong?" Holt raked a concerned gaze over her. "You're bleeding."

She glanced down at her right knee. He was right, both

knees were scraped raw and bleeding, but the right one had a far deeper gash. "Yeah, I fell."

"While playing baseball?" He looked confused.

"No, because someone threw a baseball at me as I was running." She moved past him. "Those boys had better aim than I would have given them credit for."

"I have a first aid kit and an ice pack." Holt stood close to her side as she unlocked her door. "Why don't you let me clean up those wounds?"

"Thanks, but I'm pretty sure I can manage. I'm a nurse, remember?" She wanted to let Holt take care of her, but she knew she had to resist.

"Are you hungry? I made a pot of chili. It's not half bad, if I say so myself."

Again, she felt herself weaken. She really wanted to let him clean up her knees and feed her.

When had she gotten so needy? She'd broken things off with Greg a little over five months ago, she didn't need to get involved with someone else.

Especially a resident she worked with.

"Please? It's no fun eating alone."

And just like that, she caved. "All right. Thanks."

She pushed open her apartment door and limped inside to her sofa.

As Holt elevated her feet on pillows, she knew she was in big trouble.

Fighting her attraction to Holt was proving impossible.

KRISTIN'S right knee was swollen, but the scrapes themselves weren't too bad. Still, he didn't hesitate to fetch his first aid kit and towels from his apartment, grabbing a bag of lima beans from the freezer on the way, before returning to her place.

Inwardly, he was furious a couple of kids thought it would be funny to hit a jogger with a baseball. What if they'd had hit her in the head? A head injury was no laughing matter. He thought it would be a good idea to report this to the police but sensed Kristin wouldn't go there.

"Here, hold this on your swollen knee while I get soap and water." He gently set the frozen bag of veggies on her knee.

"Lima beans? Seriously? No one eats lima beans."

"Exactly. That's why they're perfect for functioning as an ice pack." He filled a bowl with water and set it beside the washcloths and towels.

"You could use my towels," she protested as he went to work.

"No need. This is going to sting."

She sucked in a breath but didn't flinch as he gently cleaned the dirt and bits of gravel from her wounds. When he finished, he replaced the lima bean ice pack on her knee.

"Thanks, Holt." Her smile was wan, and he knew that she was still hurting.

"Do you have any ibuprofen?"

"Yes." She gestured behind her. "In the medicine cabinet."

He retrieved the over-the-counter medication and brought three tablets and a glass of water to her. She downed the meds without hesitation.

"Thanks again. You've really gone above and beyond the call of duty."

He knelt beside her, meeting her gaze. "If this knee doesn't look better by tomorrow, you shouldn't work."

Her eyes widened in horror. "No way am I calling in sick. I'm still new, haven't reached my six-month probationary period yet. I'm sure I'll be fine."

It was tempting to argue, but he decided to wait and see how the knee looked after being iced for a while. He rose to his feet. "Stay put, I'll bring over the pot of chili."

Without waiting for her to refuse, he quickly put the antiseptic and supplies back in his makeshift first aid kit and then dumped the soapy water in the sink.

Minutes later, he returned to Kristin's apartment carrying the large Crock-Pot of chili. He'd gone a little overboard, making a double batch. Deep down, he'd been hoping to share it with Kristin.

He couldn't stop thinking about her.

"Smells great," Kristin said encouragingly.

"It's my grandmother's recipe." He didn't bother pointing out that his mother had decided cooking was beneath her. His dad didn't seem to mind taking a turn in the kitchen however, and his father's mother had been more than willing to share her culinary secrets.

Kristin shifted on the sofa, emitting a soft groan. He frowned. "Are you okay?"

"My back hurts where the ball hit me." She gingerly turned so she was facing him.

"Maybe I should take a look."

"No!" She looked alarmed at his suggestion.

"You're wearing sports gear, and I'm a doctor," he pointed out. "You could have a large hematoma back there."

She hesitated, then nodded. "Okay, you can look. Feels like there's a bruise on my lower back, on the right."

He gently lifted the edge of her shirt, keeping his gaze on her pale skin. He let out a low whistle. "There's a six-centimeter round bruise that's already turning dark."

"Let me guess, the size of a baseball, right?"

"Yes." He lowered the hem of her running shirt. "I think you should call the police."

"And report what? A kid with a lousy arm accidentally hit me with a ball? Not happening." She shifted again on the sofa. "Listen, I'd like to take a shower before we eat. I'm all sweaty."

He nodded and held out his hand. "Here, lean on me."

She took his hand, her palm warm in his. He eased her upright, then slid his arm around her waist.

"You'll regret getting so close," she warned. "I'm sure I stink."

"I don't mind."

She leaned on him, limping less obviously as they made their way down the short hall to the bathroom. She paused in the doorway, glancing up at him. "I'll take it from here."

"Sure." He reluctantly released her. "But shout out if you need something."

He returned to the kitchen, taking a moment to stir the chili, then searching her cupboards for bowls and silverware. When he realized he'd forgotten the oyster crackers and white cheddar cheese, he went back to his place.

It would have been easier to have Kristin come to his apartment, but he didn't mind. Any time he was able to spend with Kristin was worth the inconvenience.

When he opened his apartment door with the crackers in hand to take back to Kristin, he stopped short when he saw Lana standing there.

"Hi, Holt."

He stepped forward, pulling the apartment door closed behind him. He wasn't the least bit interested in whatever Lana was trying to sell. "Hey, sorry, but this isn't a good time."

"Really." Her gaze took in the bag of oyster crackers and shredded cheese. "I see you've made your grandmother's famous chili."

"As I said, this isn't a good time." He tried to edge past her.

"You're going over to take care of Kristin Page, aren't you?" Lana's tone was thick with resentment. "What does she have that I don't?"

"Integrity." The word popped out of his mouth before he could stop it.

Lana sucked in a breath of outrage, but he didn't stick around to watch her explode. Instead, he hurried down to Kristin's apartment, opened the door, and stepped inside.

It wasn't until he'd set the food on her kitchen counter that Lana's words sank into his brain.

You're going over to take care of Kristin Page, aren't you?

Take care of her? How had Lana known about Kristin's injury? There would be no way for her to have known, unless she'd been there.

As an observer? Or a perpetrator?

10

Holt tried to think of a plausible reason that Lana Reasby would have known about Kristin's injury, but he couldn't come up with anything.

She had to have been in the park. Either watching or maybe encouraging the kids to take a dare.

He wanted to ask Kristin if she saw anyone who looked like Lana at the park but decided it might be best to wait until after dinner.

No point ruining her appetite.

Kristin emerged from her shower twenty minutes later, dressed in casual fleece pants and a baggy shirt. She smiled, and he was glad to see the tiny brackets of pain at the corners of her mouth were gone.

"The hot water did wonders for my sore muscles," she declared. "I feel so much better."

"Glad to hear it." He gestured to the table. "Food is ready when you are."

"I'm starving," she admitted, sinking into a chair.

"Good, because I have a lot of chili here." He dished up a heaping serving of chili in a bowl and handed it to her, then pushed the shredded cheese and crackers toward her. "Add as much as you'd like."

She ate with gusto. "This is really good. Your grandmother's recipe? I bet your mom made it for you all the time."

"Actually, my dad did most of the cooking." He offered a wry smile. "My mother's idea of cooking was ordering out."

"I see." He wondered if she was mentally comparing Heidi to his mother, an appropriate description. "You must be like your dad, then."

"I hope so." He certainly didn't think he was as high maintenance as his mother and sister. "I consider that a compliment."

She eyed him curiously across the table. "Do you mind if I ask you a question?"

"Of course not."

"Are your parents still together?"

He was surprised but nodded. "Yeah, they are. My dad is a great guy, and he loves my mother, even though I know she drives him crazy. Why do you ask?"

"I don't know, it just seems like they're very different. Kind of like you and Heidi."

It was the first time she'd brought up his sister on her own, and he wasn't sure if that was good or bad. "They are, but I guess they've managed to find some common ground." Mostly he knew their relationship had lasted this long because his father was easygoing and let many of his mother's comments slide off his shoulders.

It was a role he'd soon realized he'd be stuck in if he'd stayed with Lana. She'd sucked the life out of him at every turn, until he'd dreaded seeing her. His father might be a saint, but Holt wanted something more than tolerance from a marriage.

He wanted mutual respect, a partnership, love, and honor.

"That was delicious." Kristin pushed her bowl away with a satisfied sigh. "Any chance you'd be willing to share your grandmother's secret recipe?"

"I might," he agreed, taking another spoonful. "Do you have a family recipe to exchange in return? I'm getting tired of my meager selections."

"I have a parmesan chicken bake that's pretty good." Her gray-brown-green eyes twinkled. "I'd be willing to swap."

"Sold." He finished his meal, then rose to his feet to clear the table. When she struggled to stand, he gently rested a hand on her shoulder. "Stay there, I'll manage."

"But you cooked." Her protest made him smile. "It's only fair I clean up."

"Next time. For now, you need to rest that knee."

"The lima beans are warm."

He went over to pluck the bag off and stuck it in the freezer. "It will be ready shortly."

"Who would have thought lima beans would make a good ice pack?"

"Peas work too, but I like peas, whereas no one likes lima beans."

"Someone must or they wouldn't sell them." She laughed again, and he was glad she was feeling so much better. Maybe she'd make it to work the following morning after all. There was no denying that he'd miss her if she couldn't make it in.

Sharing a meal like this with her was so nice, he hated the idea of ruining things by bringing up his exchange with Lana. But if there was any chance his ex was involved in the baseball incident, he needed Kristin to be on alert.

And to absolutely call the police to report what happened.

When her kitchen was clean, Holt helped Kristin move over to the sofa. "Listen, there's something we need to talk about."

He felt her tense. "Like what?"

Sinking down beside her, he reached over to take her hand in his. "Tell me again about what happened on your run. Start at the beginning, if you don't mind."

"Well, it was more of a jog than a run, it's just something I do to try and stay in shape."

"Hey, any exercise is good, right?"

"Right. I ran down the road away from the apartment complex, then turned right so I could run past the park."

"And that's when you saw the two kids playing baseball?"

"Yes, two boys, maybe early teens, tossing the ball high in the air, then diving under it to catch it as if they were practicing being in the outfield. Anyway, I don't even think they noticed when I ran past, they were pretty engrossed in what they were doing."

"Were there other people in the park?"

"Yes, a couple of women were walking through."

His pulse spiked. "Blonde, brunette?"

She wrinkled her forehead trying to think. "A redhead and a blonde. Honestly, I didn't pay much attention. I was too busy trying to breathe."

He smiled and nodded. "How far did you run?"

"Not very, roughly a mile before I turned around to come back. The park was empty on the return trip, no one in sight."

He found that interesting. "No indication of who threw the baseball?"

"Nope. Again, I'm sure it was the boys hiding and throwing the ball at a passing runner as a practical joke."

"Or on a dare."

Her brow furrowed. "Who would dare them to do something like that?"

"Lana and Paulette." The redhead and the blonde, he thought darkly. "They must have recognized you."

"Come on, Holt, that's a farfetched theory."

He shook his head. "Lana showed up at my apartment when I ran over to pick up the cheese and crackers. I told her it wasn't a good time, and she accused me of heading over to take care of you."

Kristin's jaw dropped. "She said that?"

"Yeah, I don't think she meant to let that slip, but she was mad I wasn't interested in talking to her. How did she know you needed to be taken care of if she hadn't been there to see you get hit by the baseball in the first place?"

Kristin looked dazed. "I—can't believe it. She was at the park and convinced the kids to hit me with the ball?"

"Or she threw it herself, although I doubt she has the skill hit you while you were running. Either way, what happened to you was no accident."

"I guess not." She stared blindly past him as if reliving those moments when the ball hit her, knocking her off balance. "If she was involved in the baseball incident, then she and Lana must have been in the red Corvette that tried to run us off the road the other night."

"Yes. Lana and Paulette are friends. I could easily see them conspiring together to do something like this."

"Crazy behavior for a couple of highly educated residents."

"Very true." He thought back on how Lana had acted when they'd dropped off their patient in the emergency department. "Although being smart doesn't equate to having good old- fashioned common sense."

She snorted. "It's more likely that those two women aren't used to hearing the word no. They seem like the type to get by on their looks alone."

"Maybe." He shifted so he could face her. "You need to report this to the police. The baseball incident along with being run off the road both have to be on file, in case something else happens."

The light in her eyes dimmed as the realization hit. "You think they are going to try something again?"

He winced. "I think they might try something again. And if they do, I want the police to take it seriously."

There was another long silence as she digested the possibility. "Okay, fine. I'll file a report, even though there's nothing the police can do about it now."

He handed her his phone. "Better to be safe than sorry."

As he listened to Kristin's one-sided conversation with the Brookland Police Department, he knew he needed to come up with a way to convince Lana and Paulette to knock it off.

Before someone was seriously hurt.

THE FOLLOWING MORNING, Kristin's knee was still a little swollen, so she wrapped it with an Ace bandage and gamely headed to work. This time, she insisted on driving herself.

Holt had looked hurt by her decision, but he hadn't argued.

As it was, he ended up driving behind her the entire way to the Lifeline hangar, which only made her feel foolish.

Even though they'd driven in separate cars, they still walked in together.

She really, really needed to switch her schedule around so she wasn't working every single shift with Holt Baxter.

Reese was the pilot on duty that day; Megan had apparently worked the night shift. Jared O'Connor was also in the debriefing room, and she was surprised to learn he'd worked a night shift with Jenna Reed. "Good morning," she greeted them.

"Morning." Jared nodded at her, then looked at Holt. "How do you feel about picking up days tomorrow?"

"Not a problem." Holt took a seat next to Jared. "Rough night?"

"Not bad. A few calls, but nothing too crazy." Jared glanced at Jenna. "You managed to get some studying done, right?"

"Right." Jenna blushed as if she'd been caught in the act of doing something bad. "I appreciate you allowing me to do homework between calls."

"Why not? No different than playing cribbage." Jared's grin made Kristin wince. He didn't have hidden cameras posted in the lounge, did he?

"Jared, do you have a minute to talk, privately?"

Holt's seemingly innocuous request put her on high alert. "If that discussion involves me, I'd like to be included."

Holt hesitated, then shrugged. "Fine."

Jared glanced between the two of them, then rose to his feet. "My office."

Kristin wasn't happy about Holt's decision to bring Jared in on the two incidents that had taken place over the past week. At the very least, he could have warned her about his plan.

"Everything okay?" Jared's question was wary.

"You need to know that Paulette Yost and Lana Reasby have lashed out at Kristin twice now."

Jared frowned. "Lashed out, how?"

"They tried to run us off the road a few days ago when we were returning to the Crossroads with Chinese takeout. Then yesterday someone threw a baseball at Kristin as she was out jogging past the park. Thankfully, she wasn't hurt too badly."

"Someone?" Jared lifted a brow. "Kids maybe?"

"Maybe." Kristin wasn't about to stand there while Holt did all the talking. "But I saw a redhead and a blonde in the park as I ran past, along with two boys playing baseball. When I returned about twenty minutes later, the park was empty, yet someone chucked a baseball at me, hitting me in the back with enough force to knock me to the ground."

Jared's scowl deepened as he turned back to Holt. "And you think the blonde and the redhead were Paulette and her friend Lana?"

"I do." Holt spoke with conviction. "Because Lana stopped up to see me less than an hour later. When I told her it wasn't a good time, she made a snide remark about how I was too busy because I had to take care of Kristin."

"Take care of her?" Jared nodded. "Interesting choice of words."

"She was upset and spoke without thinking." Holt gestured to her. "Take a look at Kristin's right knee, it took the brunt of the fall."

"I'm fine." Kristin was growing annoyed. "And really, as you can see, we don't have any proof. Even the cops weren't interested, although they did take my report."

"I need you to both be careful." Jared's tone was serious. "Earlier this year one of the residents was being stalked by her ex-husband, and he used a rifle to shoot at the helicopter. It was only because of Reese's amazing skill that they didn't crash."

She'd heard about that, and the idea of being in a helicopter that was hit by a bullet made her shiver. Glancing at Holt, she could tell the story had hit him hard, too.

"We will be on the lookout for anything unusual," Holt finally said. "You may want to alert the rest of the staff to do the same. Paulette was particularly irritated with Ivan Ames."

"Ivan called off the last two nights because his daughter Bethany has been sick. They've started her on antibiotics, and he claims she's good enough that he can work tonight." Jared hesitated, then added, "I'll send out an email alert, but I'd like you to spread the word, too. Reading work email isn't always at the top of the priority list."

"We will," Kristin said. "Thanks for understanding."

Jared raked her with his gaze. "You sure your knee is up to working a full twelve-hour shift?"

"Absolutely." No way was she abandoning her shift when they were already short-staffed because of Paulette being removed from the program. "I'll be fine."

"Okay, then." Jared yawned and rubbed his eyes. "I need to get home. Keep me posted on anything that seems the least bit suspicious."

"Of course." Holt nodded in agreement.

Kristin didn't say anything to Holt as they returned to the debriefing room. Swallowing her annoyance, she listened to the potential transfer Jenna was telling them about.

"As soon as a bed opens in the surgical intensive care unit at Trinity, they're going to approve the transfer, so be ready. Green Bay is a long trip."

Great, just what she needed, a thirty-minute flight with

Holt. The only upside of a trip that long is that she'd be able to rest and elevate her knee, at least on the ride up to Green Bay. Not so much on the way back home.

After Jenna, Jared, and Megan were gone, Holt leaned close. "Why are you upset with me?"

She had to give him points for being perceptive. "You could have mentioned your plan to tell Jared my problems."

"Our problems, Kristin. I'm the one they're mad at. You just happen to be collateral damage. They're lashing out at you because I care about you."

Her resentment softened. It wasn't easy to stay upset with him. "You still should have told me so we could've gone in together."

"Would you have gone with me without an argument?"

She was about to agree but realized he was right. "No, probably not. But then again, being reminded of how Samantha Jarvis's ex-husband had taken a shot at the Lifeline chopper made me realize it was the right thing to do."

"Yeah." Holt looked thoughtful. "I don't think Lana or Paulette own a gun."

"Don't joke about it," she cautioned, glancing at Reese. He was on the phone, likely talking to his wife. "Besides, don't you think Lana and Paulette will move on? I mean, why would they continue to lash out at me? At us?"

Holt shrugged and shook his head. "I'm not sure, other than they must be able to tell how much I care about you."

Her heart did a funny little flop in her chest. She was trying hard to keep Holt in the friendship bucket, but when he made statements like that, her resistance melted faster than butter on a hot day.

"Don't say that." Her protest sounded pathetically feeble even to her own ears. "We work together, remember?"

"Only for the next three months." He grinned. "After

that, you'll have no excuse."

She was afraid he was right. She already liked him. Enjoyed spending time with him. No man had ever cooked for her, certainly not Greg, and she very much wanted to believe that Holt was more like his father than his mother.

And nothing like Heidi.

"Will you have dinner with me tonight?" Holt's deep husky voice made her shiver. "We can order pizza or have leftover chili."

"Who thinks about dinner at eight o'clock in the morning?"

"I do, but only because I want to spend the evening with you."

"Holt . . ." her voice trailed off. What could she say to deter him? Especially when she wanted to spend time with him, too. "Okay, dinner. We can eat leftovers, no sense in paying for pizza."

"I don't mind, you're worth it." His voice dipped lower, and she couldn't tear her gaze from his. "You're so beautiful. I think Greg Zeman is a complete idiot."

Her breath caught in her throat, and she found herself leaning toward him as he lowered his head to hers.

He kissed her sweetly, then deepened the kiss, making her ache with need. When their pagers went off, she wanted to toss the stupid thing across the room.

But she broke away from his embrace, doing her best to focus on the message displayed on the screen.

"The Green Bay transfer is on. We need to go." She rose to her feet, trying not to show how much she'd been impacted by his kiss.

This time, she was saved by the pager. But it was getting harder and harder to ignore her growing feelings for him.

She could only hope Holt Baxter didn't break her heart.

11

It took the entire flight to Green Bay for Holt to recover from Kristin's brief but heated kiss enough to center his mind on patient care.

He was thrilled to know they'd be sharing dinner after work. He had no idea why she'd changed her mind, but he was happy she had.

On one hand, he could understand her reluctance to become involved with another resident after the way her former fiancé, Greg, had cheated on her. But Kristin was smart, she had to know that most guys didn't do that. Most guys didn't lie and cheat on their girlfriends, fiancées, or wives.

His sister, Heidi, had certainly become bitter after the breakup of her marriage. With good reason, but he'd often wished Heidi would seek professional help to get over what had happened. His sister needed to move on with her life, not wallow in the past.

Easier said than done. He wasn't trying to make light of what his sister and Kristin had gone through. But hanging on to deep resentment and bitter anger wasn't healthy.

And he was worried about Heidi. He'd tried to call her last night, but she hadn't answered. He made a mental note to try her again soon.

When they were fifteen minutes from Green Bay, Holt contacted the hospital ICU doctor to get an update on their patient's condition. Their patient was a twenty-six-year-old woman named Joyce Winter with graft vs. host disease after a bone marrow transplant. It was a horrible complication, where the patient's immune system actually began to attack the newly transplanted bone marrow. He knew the survival rates were low, but Joyce had youth on her side. She'd apparently had her original care provided at Trinity Medical Center but had returned home to live with her mother in Green Bay after the initial transplant.

Holt learned her vitals were stable but that she was intubated on a ventilator and had a critically low white blood cell count and platelet count. He knew one of the biggest threats they'd face during their flight back to Milwaukee was bleeding.

"ETA three minutes," Reese said.

Holt glanced at Kristin. She'd kept her knee elevated during the flight, but she was now moving the joint a bit as if relieving the stiffness. "Sure you're okay?"

"Fine." She waved off his concern. "Let's do this."

Reese landed the chopper on the rooftop landing pad. Holt jumped out first to go around to the back. Kristin pushed the gurney toward him, then jumped down from the helicopter. He thought he noticed a slight wince marring her features, but she didn't show any sign of pain when she joined him.

They wheeled the gurney inside and removed their helmets. Kristin's dark hair was pulled back in a ponytail, wisps framing her face.

They made their way to the third-floor intensive care unit and found Joyce readily enough.

Holt came up to stand beside the attending physician. "Any changes since we last spoke?"

"No. We've given a pack of platelets and have a second one for you to take during transport." Dr. O'Grady gestured to the bed. "She's begun to ooze from her nose and mouth."

Just as he'd feared, but Holt nodded. "I'll gladly take the platelets. What about cryo and fresh frozen plasma?"

O'Grady hesitated, then nodded. "Noreen, will you call down to the blood bank for a pack of cryoprecipitate and two units of fresh frozen plasma for bed six?"

"Of course." The woman seated behind the desk lifted her phone and dialed the lab.

"Thanks." Holt watched as Kristin and the bedside nurse switched Joyce from the hospital equipment to the portable devices used by Lifeline. "Anything else I should be aware of?"

There was a slight hesitation before O'Grady responded. "Some interesting family dynamics between the girl's mother and father. They're divorced, and the two of them can't be in the room at the same time without screaming at each other. We put them on alternating visiting hours: mom gets even hours and dad gets odd hours. Frankly, the mother is crazy. The girl's dad is far more reasonable about the chances of his daughter beating this. Mom, not so much."

Holt nodded. "I'll be sure to pass that information along to the MICU attending on duty."

The words had barely left his mouth when a woman began screeching. "Noo! You can't take my baby!"

Just as Kristin was connecting Joyce's chest leads, a woman rushed up and threw herself over the patient as if protecting her from a grizzly attack rather than an attempt to transfer her to a higher level of care.

"Margaret, please, you have to stay back." The bedside nurse vainly attempted to pull the wailing woman off Joyce's body.

The monitor began to alarm. Other nurses came over to help pull Joyce's mother away, one of them shouting for security.

Holt tried to stay out of the Green Bay Hospital staff's way, instead focusing on Kristin's attempt to get the patient reconnected. "Is her heart rate really that high?"

"I don't know." Kristin's tone was laced with frustration. "There's too much artifact to get a good view of the EKG strip."

It took four staff members and the security guard to pull Margaret off her daughter. Once they were clear, Joyce's heart rhythm settled in.

"That's better," Kristin murmured. Holt nodded, taking note of Joyce's pulse of 96 beats per minute. "Although her blood pressure has dropped a bit."

Holt had no idea if the patient's vitals were in response to her mother's outburst or a symptom of something else. He turned toward O'Grady. "Have you needed vasopressors?"

"On and off, yes." O'Grady frowned at the vitals displayed on their portable equipment. "I've been using vasopressin, but it's been off for about three hours now. We can put up another bag for the transfer."

"Yes, that would be good." Considering the thirty-minute flight before them, Holt wasn't about to take any chances.

It took another fifteen minutes for the vasopressin, the cryoprecipitate, and the fresh frozen plasma to arrive. Once

Kristin had the vasopressin connected to Joyce's IV, he gave the signal to go.

"We'll infuse the platelets and cryo on the way."

"Okay." Kristin didn't argue. She tucked the edges of a blanket securely around Joyce's body, then gave the gurney a push. "I'm ready if you are."

Together they wheeled Joyce out of the ICU and toward the elevator that would take them up to the rooftop landing pad. Thankfully, there was no sign of her mother, although he didn't doubt the woman would be driving down to Trinity Medical Center as soon as possible.

Everyone handled grief differently, but it was hard to understand how a mother could put her daughter's life at risk like that. Wasn't his problem, but it would certainly impact Joyce's care when she arrived in the ICU.

When it came time to lift the gurney through the back hatch, he took most of the weight in an effort to avoid undue pressure on Kristin's injured knee. Five minutes later, they were in the air.

"Joyce, can you hear me? You're in the Lifeline helicopter on your way to Trinity Medical Center." Kristin's voice was calm and soothing. "We're going to take good care of you, okay?"

Joyce gave a faint nod. Talking wasn't possible with her breathing tube connected to their portable ventilator. Her vitals had stabilized, giving hope that this would be an uneventful flight.

Kristin jotted notes on a clipboard, then began to infuse the platelets. Once those were in, she quickly hung the cryo-precipitate.

Just as he was settling back to enjoy the ride, Joyce began to cough. Kristin quickly opened a suction kit and began to help clear out the ETT.

But the secretions were bloody. His chest squeezed with fear, and he leaned forward to see better. He cued his mic, making sure the patient couldn't overhear their conversation, then asked, "She's bleeding?"

"Yes." Kristin's green-gray-brown eyes were grave.

"Let me suction her, you set up the two units of fresh frozen plasma."

Kristin nodded and stripped off her gloves, then opened another sterile suction kit for him. She hung the fresh frozen plasma on the same line as the cryo.

More blood came from her ETT tube, and he quelled a flash of panic as he did his best to clear her airway. "Reese? What's our ETA?"

"Twenty minutes, I'm bucking up against a stern headwind."

Twenty minutes. His stomach knotted, and he felt sweat dampen his brow.

Joyce was bleeding from deep in her lungs, and there was nothing he could do to stop it.

Except hope and pray Reese got them to Trinity Medical Center before she went into full-blown cardiac arrest.

KRISTIN INFUSED the fresh frozen plasma as fast as it would go, knowing there wasn't anything else they could do to prevent Joyce from bleeding out.

Twenty minutes seemed far too long. "Reese, we may have to divert to the closest hospital."

"Ten-four. Just let me know when," Reese answered.

"Divert to another hospital?" Holt glanced at her, frank hope lighting up his eyes. "That sounds like a good idea. What are we waiting for?"

She hated to burst his bubble. "We can divert to the closest hospital, but all the facilities en route will be small community hospitals, not tertiary care centers." She shook her head. "Her best chance of survival is for us to get her to Trinity Medical Center. They have the most expertise with this kind of thing."

He grimaced and nodded. "Understood." He suctioned her one more time, then reconnected Joyce to the ventilator. Together, they watched her pulse oximeter hover in the high eighties.

"I'm not sure what else to do." Holt's frank admission surprised her. "If the platelets, cryo, and plasma don't work, I'm out of ideas."

"Look, she's back up to ninety percent." She hated seeing Holt so defeated. She didn't know many residents who took their patients' outcomes so personally. As if each one who didn't do well was a personal failure on his part.

She admired his tenacity and dedication to his patients. A flashing light caught her eye, and she noticed Joyce's blood pressure was dipping down again.

"Increase the vasopressin drip to keep her MAP at sixty."

Following Holt's order, she increased the drip. But the drop in blood pressure was concerning. It made her worry that Joyce was bleeding internally from other sources.

Moving the blanket aside, she did a quick abdominal exam. There were no obvious signs of bleeding, but she didn't find that reassuring.

"What's wrong?"

She forced a smile and shook her head. "Nothing. Just worried about internal bleeding."

"Me, too."

Kristin switched her mic to communicate with Joyce. "Joyce, are you feeling okay? Any pain?"

Joyce opened her eyes, but her gaze was unfocused. She shook her head, although Kristin wasn't sure which question she was responding to, then her eyelids drifted closed.

"ETA fourteen minutes."

Reese's update didn't help her relax. The time had never dragged by as slowly as it did now.

Joyce's blood pressure dropped again, so she increased the drip.

"The vasopressin may help clamp down on any bleeders," Holt murmured.

"Yeah, I know." It was true, although she knew that there were side effects from being on high doses of vasopressors, too. Joyce's hands were icy cold, so she tucked them beneath the blanket.

Come on, she silently urged. *We need you to hang on just a little while longer.*

Joyce's blood pressure stabilized, but she didn't dare breathe a sigh of relief. The minutes ticked by more slowly than ever before. When Reese informed them they were five minutes out, she glanced over at Holt.

"We can do this." His tone was encouraging despite looking just as grim as she felt. "Reese? I'm requesting a hot unload. I'd like the ICU team to meet us on the helipad."

"Ten-four." Reese relayed the message.

Joyce's blood pressure remained in the 90/60 range, but only because she was close to being maxed out on the vasopressin. "Should I get another vasopressor ready to go?"

Holt hesitated, then nodded. "Let's start Levophed."

She grimaced but prepared the drip as he'd requested. In the ICU, she and the other nurses often referred to Levophed as *leave them dead* because it was often used in a last-ditch effort to save a patient's life.

But today, a touch of Levophed worked to bring Joyce's blood pressure from 88 systolic up to 96 systolic.

Reese banked the chopper toward Trinity. As he brought the helicopter down gently on the landing pad, she could see a bevy of nurses and doctors waiting for them near the doorway.

Without wasting a second, Holt jumped down and ran around to the back. In moments, they had the gurney out of the helicopter and wheeling toward the healthcare team.

Holt updated Charles Ashe, the physician on duty, as to Joyce's change in condition during the flight. When they reached the ICU, wheeling Joyce into one of the open bedsides, Kristin couldn't deny a wave of relief.

They'd made it without losing her. Their twenty-six-year-old patient was still very sick, but Kristin knew deep in her heart that this was where she belonged. The team here at Trinity offered the best chance at survival.

They'd barely gotten her switched off the equipment when they received another call.

Nothing boring about this shift, that was for sure.

The call was related to a high-speed crash on the interstate, leaving one driver dead and the other severely injured.

The flight to the crash scene didn't take too long. Her right knee gave a sharp twang when she jumped down from the helicopter. It hadn't been too sore this morning, but she could tell it was swelling as her shift went on.

"Hurts?"

Holt was far too observant. She shrugged. "A little, but nothing I can't handle."

As they ran the gurney over to where the firefighters and paramedics were gathered, she could see they were still attempting to free the driver from the vehicle that was squashed like a bug.

"Can I help?" Being smaller than most of the guys, she was often able to get into vehicles to offer assistance where they couldn't.

"Would be nice to get a set of vitals," the paramedic to her right said.

"Okay." She began to crawl in through the busted window on the passenger side. The driver was unconscious but breathing on his own, a good sign.

There wasn't much room, but she managed to kneel on the passenger seat to place her fingers along the driver's neck to feel for his pulse. It was fast and thready. She counted the beats, then reported, "He's tachy at one sixteen; he needs fluids."

"Can you start an IV?" Holt was at the passenger window with their duffel bag of supplies.

"I think so."

He handed her the IV catheter. She placed the IV in the driver's forearm, then connected the tubing Holt handed to her. "Thanks. Now I need a blood pressure cuff."

Holt handed the manual cuff through the broken window. Kneeling like this wasn't easy, but she ignored the pain. This guy needed her, and she wasn't going to let him down.

"BP is ninety over forty-eight."

"Open the fluids, he needs volume."

She did as Holt requested, then had to shift a bit to ease her weight off her knee. The team of firefighters worked with crowbars and buzz saws to get the driver's door open. She continued monitoring the driver the best she could, despite the noise.

After what seemed like forever, but was only about twenty minutes, the driver's side door abruptly opened, falling to the concrete with a loud clatter. The firefighters stepped back to give the paramedics room to work. They brought over the Lifeline gurney and moved the driver gingerly into position.

Holding the IV up with one hand, she managed to climb out behind the patient. Holt came around to meet with her, and together they performed a quick exam.

Less than a week of flying together, but they had a great working relationship, each easily falling into their respective roles.

This transport was uneventful, and when they had their injured driver safe in the trauma bay, she watched for a few minutes as the team took over.

"I can't stop thinking about Joyce," Holt said in a low voice. "Maybe we can stop up to check on her in a while."

"Of course." Some transports haunted you more than others. For her, it had been Barbie Martin. It was the first time she'd ever had a patient who died of anorexia.

She hoped and prayed Joyce Winter fared better. It wasn't good to lose a patient, but the younger ones were always so much harder to handle.

It made you face your own mortality. And forced you to realize that life is precious and should be lived to its fullest since you never knew what might happen down the road.

Surely Joyce hadn't considered she might need a bone marrow transplant, and worse that her own immune system would turn against her.

"Are you ready to go?" Holt's voice brought her back to the present. "It's been close to three hours since we dropped Joyce off in the medical ICU, and I'm curious to find out how she's doing."

"I'm ready." She took one end of the gurney. "We need to return this to the chopper first and let Reese know our plans. He may want to take the time to refuel."

"Good idea."

The trip up to the helicopter didn't take very long. They had to climb inside to tell Reese their plans, and he agreed to use the time to refuel the chopper.

Holt jumped down first, then offered his hand. She took it, mostly because her knee was throbbing in earnest now. Climbing into the passenger seat of the car had taken a toll.

Doing her best not to limp, she followed Holt into the MICU. Then nearly walked into him when he suddenly stopped.

"YOU!" a familiar screech echoed through the unit.

She stepped to the side just in time to see Joyce's mother come running toward Holt, her hands raised, fingers fisted. She attacked Holt, punching and kicking like a wild animal. *"You killed my baby!"*

12

B lows landed on his chest, his face, his shins, his abdomen, but Holt couldn't move, not even in an attempt to block her fists. The fury radiating off Joyce's mother battered his soul worse than her physical assault.

Security staff and nurses yanked Margaret off of him, holding her arms to her sides while the police were called. Still Holt didn't move, the soles of his feet seemingly glued to the floor.

Joyce had died. All-too young at twenty-six years old, she'd died two and a half hours after being transported from Green Bay to Trinity Medical Center. At some level, he couldn't blame Joyce's mother for being angry.

"Are you okay?" Kristin's voice permeated the fog of horror surrounding his brain.

"Yeah." He'd have bruises in the morning, but nothing like the heaviness that weighed on his heart. He turned toward Charles Ashe, the provider he'd spoken to when they'd brought the patient in. Before he could ask what had transpired in the time he'd been gone, Joyce's mother started up again.

"I can't leave my baby!" Margaret shrieked as the police officers began leading her away.

"Ma'am, you're under arrest for assault and battery," one of the officers informed her.

"No." Holt stepped forward, lifting a hand in protest. "It's fine. I don't want to press charges."

"Why not?" Kristin asked in a hushed tone. "She attacked you."

"Out of despair and grief." He glanced at her. "Arresting her won't change anything."

The two cops glanced at each other as if unsure of their next steps. Charles Ashe took over, giving a resigned nod. "She can spend five more minutes at her daughter's bedside, but then she'll need to leave."

A subdued Margaret was walked by the police over to her daughter's bedside. All the equipment had been disconnected, and Holt had to admit Joyce looked at peace. Her mother's sobs echoed loudly through the unit, and no one spoke for several long moments.

Finally, the officers led Margaret away, escorting her off hospital property.

Holt looked at Charles Ashe. "What happened?"

The physician sighed, his expression weary. "She began to bleed from her rectum and from her mouth. We instituted the massive transfusion protocol, but we couldn't get her stable enough to do a GI procedure. She coded, and we ended up calling it after ten minutes."

He nodded thoughtfully. There was no point in giving a never-ending supply of precious blood products if you couldn't cauterize or treat the source of the bleeding.

Frankly, he would have done the same thing if he'd been the ICU attending on duty.

"Understandable. Thanks for letting me know." Holt turned toward Kristin. "We should head back to Lifeline."

She fell into step beside him as they left the unit. "Are you sure you're okay?"

He shrugged, then rubbed a hand over his cheek where one of the blows had landed. "It's hard losing a patient. And when you look at it from her mother's perspective, we transported her child only to lose her shortly thereafter. It's a two-hour drive from Green Bay, she probably arrived just as Joyce was bleeding out in front of her eyes. That would shock anyone."

"I know, and I understand she was grieving, but it's not right that she attacked you like that." Kristin jabbed the button for the elevator. "What would you have done if she'd physically assaulted me?"

The thought brought him up short, and he realized he'd have absolutely responded differently. Not only would he have grabbed the woman and yanked her off Kristin, but he likely would have pressured Kristin into pressing charges.

"Okay, you made your point. But I can't bear to add to her stress level right now." He was anxious to change the subject. "Let's stop for lunch on the way back."

"Sounds good."

He wasn't terribly hungry, but grabbing a bite to eat offered a nice diversion from the scene in the medical intensive care unit. Never in his life had a patient's family member physically attacked him, and he hoped that was the first and last time he'd experience something like that.

"There's a deli across the street from Lifeline that offers a nice variety of sandwiches," Kristin said as they made their way through the hospital lobby. "There's also a pizza joint."

"Let's try the deli." He lightly rested his hand in the small of Kristin's back as they walked into the cool October air. The clouds dotted the sky without the threat of rain.

Wait a minute, was he seriously wishing for bad weather to avoid being called out for a trauma or a transfer? He shook off the lingering feeling of failure. Logically, he knew that even if Joyce hadn't been transferred to Trinity Medical Center, her outcome would have been the same. No reason for him to take her death so personally.

"I'm having the turkey avocado sandwich with a cup of soup," Kristin said. "What about you?"

"The roast beef." He pulled his wallet out of the back pocket of his flight suit. "Lunch is on me."

Kristin rolled her eyes. "Nope. We each pay our own way while we're working." She managed to pay for her meal before he could stop her.

He tried not to feel hurt, despite knowing she was right. As much as he was falling for her, they should keep things professional while they were working.

Besides, she'd agreed to have dinner with him after work, so he couldn't complain. In fact, it was the one thing he was genuinely looking forward to.

They were able to finish their lunch without being interrupted by a call. As they walked back to the Lifeline hangar, Kristin abruptly stopped.

"Did you forget something?"

She slowly shook her head. "Isn't that Paulette's Corvette parked between your truck and my car?"

He frowned. "Looks like it. Maybe she's trying to convince Jared to take her back."

"I don't think he'd do that, would he?" She resumed walking, albeit more slowly than before, as if she dreaded the thought of running into Paulette.

"Highly doubtful." Jared seemed to be the kind of guy who stuck to his guns, regardless of outside pressure. Which made him wonder if Ben Harris, the medical director of the Trinity Emergency Department, might have reached out to Jared on Paulette's behalf.

"Maybe we should go back to the deli for a while." Kristin hunched her shoulders and tucked a strand of her hair behind her ear. "I'm not in the mood for another confrontation."

He couldn't blame her—it had already been an emotionally gut-wrenching day. "Fine with me."

They turned away, but by the time they'd arrived at the deli, he heard the roar of a car engine. From the corner of his eye, he saw a flash of red as the Corvette drove off.

"It's safe now." As he spoke, their pagers went off.

The rest of the day went by quickly and without family drama. The only bad news was the preliminary autopsy report on the fifteen-year-old who'd fallen off the roof of the high school. The ME's office was deeming the boy's death a suicide, based on his having previous suicide attempts and pending the results of the tox screen.

Dead at fifteen. It was difficult to wrap his head around it, but he forced himself to focus on the present.

There was nothing he could do about what happened in the past, but he absolutely needed to take care of the future. He'd wanted a chance to speak to Jared about Paulette's visit, but the medical director was gone by the time they returned.

Kristin reported off to the incoming shift, and he was glad to see that Ivan had returned and was paired up with Matt. His phone rang, and he was surprised to see his sister's name on the screen.

"Excuse me." He lifted the phone to his ear and left the

debriefing room for privacy. "Heidi, where have you been? I've been worried about you."

"I haven't felt much like talking." Heidi's voice was thick with tears. "But I can't be here alone any longer. Will you please stop by after work tonight?"

He closed his eyes and inwardly groaned. "I have a date tonight, but I'm off tomorrow. Why don't we get together then?"

"A date? With who? I thought you broke up with what's-her-name."

"Lana, and yes, I did. I'm seeing a flight nurse now. Kristin Page. You might remember her from high school; we worked at Carlson's Custard together."

"Prissy Krissy? You've got to be kidding me. Come on, Holt, you can do so much better than that."

His sister's acidic tone made him grind his teeth together. "Stop it. She's beautiful, smart, and an excellent flight nurse."

For a long moment Heidi didn't respond, but when she did, her tone was quiet. "So that's it? You're going to ignore my needs because you have a date?"

He suppressed a sigh. "Heidi, we can get together tomorrow, okay? I'll drive out to your place mid-morning."

"Trent and his new fiancée have set a wedding date." Heidi's stark tone was raw with emotion. "Valentine's Day. Can you believe it? That's barely four months away. I just know she's pregnant."

Oh boy, no wonder Heidi was on edge. "I'm sorry to hear that. I'm sure it's not going to be easy for you."

"You think?" Her tone dripped with bitterness.

Holt hesitated, wondering if he should ask Kristin for a rain check on dinner. She probably wouldn't mind. But he quickly decided against it. This day had been long enough, he wasn't sure he had the emotional energy to deal with Heidi on top of what he'd already been through.

"Tomorrow, okay?" he repeated. "I'll call you before I head out."

"Fine." Her clipped tone told him she was upset. "Goodbye."

He stared down at his phone screen for a long moment, feeling guilty and wondering if he should call her back. But he slipped the phone into his pocket and returned to the debriefing room.

He'd face Heidi tomorrow, maybe find a way to convince her to seek professional help. She couldn't keep falling apart every time her ex-husband did something. Especially if his soon-to-be wife really was pregnant. Learning about the birth of their baby might send Heidi off the deep end.

Kristin came out of the debriefing room, a questioning look in her eye. "Everything okay?"

"Yeah." He smiled. "Ready to go?"

"I'll meet you back at the apartment. We're having leftovers, remember? And you left the chili at my place."

"I love leftovers." He decided not to add how much he'd been looking forward to spending more time with her. Even if that meant doing nothing more than eating leftover chili

Pathetic? Maybe, but he didn't care.

He hadn't felt like this about a woman in a long time, and he wasn't about to let it go.

Now, he just needed some way to convince Kristin he was worth it.

$\sim$

KRISTIN GLANCED AT HOLT, sensing his distraction. Likely

still reeling from being physically attacked by Joyce's mother.

Crazy the way the woman had taken all her anger out on Holt. It wasn't as if he'd made the decision to transfer her daughter to Trinity. She had to give Holt extra brownie points for not pressing charges. Would she have been able to be so forgiving?

She wasn't sure.

Holt walked her to her car, waiting as always for her to get behind the wheel. "See you soon," he said before shutting her door.

With a wave, she turned the key. The engine roared to life, then coughed and sputtered, then shut down. What in the world? She tried again, still nothing. The engine wanted to start, but it wouldn't stay on, and the second attempt was even worse than the first.

A wave of despair washed over her. The car was a good ten years old, so it wasn't a complete surprise that parts might fail, but she'd just paid for her new apartment. Fixing her car wasn't part of the plan.

Holt tapped on her window. "Want me to take a look?"

She nodded and released the hood. He lifted it up and used the flashlight app on his phone to peer at her engine. His expression was perplexed when he returned to her driver's side window. "Try again."

She turned the key. The engine wouldn't start at all now. "I don't understand."

He looked the car over, then went to the gas tank. "No safety lock?"

"It's an old car. Why?"

Leaning over, he sniffed around the tank, then straightened. "I think someone may have tampered with it."

"Tampered how?"

He grimaced. "Sugar. Putting sugar in the gas tank is a sure way to ruin the engine."

"Ruin the engine? You mean my car may need a whole new engine?" She gaped at him, then remembered seeing Paulette's red Corvette earlier, parked between her car and Holt's truck. "I can't believe she'd do something like this."

"I'll drive you home. We'll deal with this tomorrow." Holt's expression was grim. "If she really did this, then the police will finally have to take action."

"Yeah, right. Because I'm sure the police will agree that simply seeing her Corvette here is proof of her guilt." She couldn't believe Paulette would be so bold as to pour sugar in her gas tank. "Why does she hate me so much? What did I do?"

"Nothing." Holt ushered her toward his truck. "I'm sorry, Kristin. It's my fault. She's lashing out at you because of me."

"I can't afford a new car." A wave of hopelessness hit hard. "And my insurance deductible is a thousand dollars." Money she didn't have after paying first month's rent along with a security deposit.

"Don't panic until we know for sure what happened." He opened the passenger-side door of his truck for her.

She slid into the seat, rubbing her sore knee and making a mental note to sign up for extra hours. It wasn't as if she didn't have some cash in her savings account, but she hadn't planned on something like this.

She sighed and tried to shake off the damage to her car during the short ride back to the Crossroads.

Holt parked in his usual spot in the underground parking lot, and they rode the elevator to the fourth floor.

She unlocked her door, but Holt kept going. "I'm going to shower and change, meet you in thirty?"

"Sure." She wouldn't mind changing out of her flight suit

too and maybe freshening up a bit. Her knee hurt, so a dose of ibuprofen was a definite must.

After a quick shower, she downed the ibuprofen, then pulled on a pair of worn jeans and a long-sleeved T-shirt, going with casual and comfy rather than fancy. Either he liked her the way she was or he didn't. During her engagement to Greg, he'd often asked her to dress nicer, a not so subtle way of pointing out she needed to look the part of being engaged to a resident, soon-to-be doctor.

No way was she going down that path again.

In the kitchen she pulled out the leftover crock of chili and spooned it into bowls to heat up in the microwave. When Holt rapped on her door, she wiped her hands on a towel and went over to let him in.

"Hey." His smile lit up his entire face, sending a sizzling awareness through her. "I brought the bag of lima beans."

That made her laugh. "Come in." Hoping her cheeks weren't too red, she stepped back to give him room to enter. "I'm warming up the food now."

"Great, happy to help." He crossed over to the counter, seemingly at home in her living space. She closed the door and locked it before joining him.

"Sit." He gestured to the chair. "Put your knee up and put the bag of frozen lima beans over it."

Since her knee was bothering her, she sat. The frozen lima beans felt good.

She watched as he finished warming up the leftover chili and brought the two bowls over to the table, along with silverware. "Dig in," he invited.

She leaned forward to do just that. His phone rang, a shrill sound in the quiet apartment. He glanced at the screen, grimaced, then hit the end button.

"Was that Jared?" She tried to sound casual, even though

she knew she was being nosy. Holt's personal calls weren't any of her business.

"No, my sister. It's fine, I spoke to her earlier."

"Heidi?" It took all of her willpower not to wrinkle her nose in distaste. High school was a long time ago, it was time to move forward. "You should call her back; it might be important."

"It's not." He took another spoonful of chili. "I already told her I'd head over to see her tomorrow, since I'm off work. Although now, I'll wait until after we take care of your car."

"Not sure there's much to do, other than have it towed to the closest garage." She spooned another bit of chili into her mouth. Even reheated it was excellent. "I don't need your help for that."

"I insist. Especially since I'm partially responsible."

"You're not." Although now that she thought about it, he kinda was. Not directly of course, Holt was too nice of a guy to do something so destructive, but she knew things might be very different if they hadn't been partnered together.

If they weren't seeing each other.

"Ah-ha. See?" He waved his spoon in the air. "You know it is my fault. Because I didn't stick up for Paulette the way Lana wanted me to."

"Listen, maybe we should slow down a bit."

He jerked his head up. "Slow down? I didn't get the impression we were in a race."

"We're not, but I think it might be better if we wait for things to settle down before being seen together in public."

"Hey, don't worry." He reached over to lightly squeeze her hand. "I'll pay for the repairs on your car."

"That's not what I meant." She blew out a frustrated

breath. "I think it's clear Lana still has feelings for you. And for whatever reason, she's decided to lash out at me."

He didn't respond right away, but then pushed his plate away and came around the table to kneel beside her. "Kristin, I care about you. A lot. I like spending time with you, and I want to be with you. Please don't let this come between us."

His green eyes were so intense, so compelling, she couldn't refuse. "All right."

Relief brightened his face. "Thank you." He leaned over and kissed her.

As much as she wanted nothing more than to melt into his arms, she forced herself to put a hand on his chest, pushing him away. "But, Holt, there has to be something we can do to convince Paulette and Lana to stop the madness. I thought the baseball incident was bad enough, but sugar in my gas tank is far worse."

"No, the baseball incident was worse, a car can be fixed, but that baseball hurt you. I'm still angry about that." His stern expression cleared. "Try not to worry, I'll see what I can do." He smiled and kissed her again. And this time, she gave up trying to resist.

Being in Holt's arms felt so right. And long after he'd gone back to his apartment, she realized that her attempt to avoid being in a relationship with Holt had failed.

She cared about him, too. Way too much.

13

Holt woke the following morning, determined to get Lana and Paulette to back off. He was scheduled to work the night shift, which meant there wasn't time to waste.

First he called a local garage to arrange for Kristin's car to be towed and evaluated. He told the mechanic about his suspicion about sugar being placed in the gas tank, and the guy let him know they'd have an estimate before noon.

When that was arranged, he called Lana. To his surprise, she answered his call. "Hi, Holt."

"Hi. I know it's last minute, but I was wondering if you're available for lunch today."

There was a brief silence before she answered. "I'm working today, but I could take a quick break to talk."

A quick break wasn't what he'd been looking for, but waiting until they both had a day off might take too long and waiting wasn't an option. This ridiculousness had to stop, now. "Okay, I'll head over to Trinity around noon and page you when I get there."

"Okay, see you then." If Lana suspected what he wanted to talk to her about, she didn't let on.

Since he didn't know Paulette's personal information, he had to call Lifeline to get her phone number from Jared.

"I can't give you that," Jared protested. "It's a breach of privacy."

"I know, but I have reason to believe she's still causing issues for Kristin. Yesterday after work, her car wouldn't start because sugar had been put into her gas tank."

"Sugar? That's been confirmed?"

He hesitated. "Not yet, but it will be. And we saw Paulette's Corvette parked near Kristin's car while we ate lunch at the deli. I'm telling you, it's no coincidence."

Jared didn't say anything for a long time. "Okay, I can see why you might be suspicious, but I don't feel good giving you her cell number."

Holt thought for a moment. "Is she still on the staff listing on the computer?"

"Possibly." Jared's tone was wary. "But if it is, I should take her off since she's no longer part of the program."

"Will you wait fifteen minutes before you do that? I'll be right there."

Jared sighed. "Okay, fine. I'll finish up the next schedule first."

"Thanks. I owe you one." Holt didn't even shower but headed straight for the Lifeline hangar. When he entered the lounge, he saw Kate sitting on the sofa while another emergency medicine resident by the name of Drake Thornton was working on the computer.

"Hey, Holt. What's up?" Kate was gregarious by nature, and while he hadn't flown with her yet, he sensed she would be one of those who talked a lot during the flight.

"Nothing much, just need to look at something on the

computer." He walked over to Drake. "Sorry to bother you, but can I take over for a few minutes? It won't take long."

Drake shrugged. "Sure." He pushed back from the computer and stood. As if on cue his pager and Kate's went off simultaneously.

"Transfer from Appleton," Kate read from her pager. "We're up, Drake. Let's go."

Seconds later, Drake and Kate were running toward the chopper. Holt quickly logged into the computer and searched out the staff listing. Relieved, he found Paulette's phone number and quickly typed it into his phone.

It was a long shot to think Paulette would join him and Lana at Trinity Medical Center for lunch, but he decided to try anyway. If she wouldn't come, he could set up something with her for a different time.

He wanted both of them to know he and Kristin were on to their shenanigans. And that he wouldn't hesitate to go to Ben Harris, the ED Medical Director, with his suspicions.

Certainly, they'd back off on the stalker-like pranks if they knew their careers were at stake.

Paulette didn't answer, so he left a message explaining he and Lana were having lunch at Trinity Medical Center around noon and were hoping she could join them. He doubted she'd come, unless her curiosity got the better of her.

Holt returned to the Crossroads in time to see Kristin coming out of the front door. When she saw his truck, she frowned and waved at him to come over.

After pressing the button to lower the passenger-side window, he caught her gaze. "What's wrong? You look upset."

"Why would you tow my car to a garage without asking

me?" She crossed her arms over her chest. "It's *my* car, Holt. I already told you I didn't want you paying for the damage."

"I'm sorry. I should have called you, but don't you think Lana and Paulette should pay for the damage?"

"Yeah, right." She scoffed. "As if they would."

He decided not to tell her his plan to meet Lana for lunch. At least, not yet. "I'm sorry," he repeated. "The garage has very reasonable prices, and I know they'll treat you fairly."

Her multicolored gaze bored into his. "Don't do that again."

He lifted his hands up in surrender. "I won't."

She muttered something under her breath that sounded like *Why don't I believe that*, but then turned to go back inside.

"Kristin, wait. Would you like a ride to the garage so you can talk to the mechanic personally?"

She hesitated, then turned to face him with a resigned look. "Yeah, okay. But I don't want to stay long, I have to cover Andrew's shift tonight, so I'd like to take a nap."

"You're working tonight?" He glanced at her, waiting until she secured her seat belt before putting the truck in gear. "So am I. It's one of Paulette's shifts."

He was disconcerted by the pained expression on her face.

"Are you upset about us working together?"

"No, but honestly, I've never worked so many shifts with one resident before."

"Maybe it's God's way of keeping us together."

A reluctant smile tugged at the corner of her mouth. "Maybe."

Personally, he was thrilled to discover he'd be flying with

Kristin again. She was an amazing nurse. Her knowledge and skill had helped him stay on track more than once.

And he liked spending time with her, too. At work, after work, or on their off day, it didn't matter.

He didn't just like her. His chest tightened as the realization hit hard.

He was totally and completely in love with her.

It was impossible for her to hang on to her anger. Holt meant well, but she wasn't used to having someone take over like that.

For all his faults, of which there were many, Greg would never have arranged a tow truck for her dead car without talking to her about it. Deep down, she doubted he would have offered to pay for it either. Maybe she was being a bit of a Pollyanna, but she couldn't help feeling touched by Holt's efforts to help her out.

Not that she needed a handout. Her parents had relocated a year or two ago to Arizona, inviting her to come along. It was a sweet offer, but she had a life here in Milwaukee, so she'd stayed behind, determined to remain independent. And she always preferred to pay her own way.

The mechanic at the garage, a guy named Timmer O'Leary, explained that indeed sugar had been poured into her gas tank.

"Unfortunately, I'll need to drop the tank, clean it out, remove and clean the fuel filter. Once that's done, I may also need to replace the fuel pump." Timmer looked apologetic. "If I need to do everything including the fuel pump, it's going to cost nearly a thousand dollars. If the fuel pump is okay, it will only be about four hundred dollars."

She forced a smile, despite the sinking feeling in her gut. "Let's hope the fuel pump is okay."

"Agree." Timmer glanced between her and Holt. "You want me to go ahead with the repairs? It will take me up to two days, depending on the fuel pump."

"Yes, please." She pulled out her checkbook, but he waved her aside.

"Let's wait to see how extensive the damage is before you pay anything. I'll be in touch when I know more."

"Thanks." She tucked the checkbook back into her purse. "You have my cell number, correct?"

Timmer nodded. After all, Holt had given him her number, which is how she'd learned of her car being towed to the garage in the first place.

"Okay, keep me posted on the status of the repairs." She turned and headed back outside. Working an extra shift tonight to cover Andrew's shift would help pay for the repairs, but it was becoming more difficult to get ahead financially.

Moving to the Crossroads might have been a mistake, but it was too late to worry about that now. She'd signed a lease committing to stay for the next year, so she wasn't going anywhere until next October.

She was so preoccupied with her financial situation, she barely noticed when Holt pulled up to the front of their apartment building.

"Thanks for the ride." She thought it was strange he hadn't pulled into the underground parking garage.

"I'm happy to drive you to work tonight, too," he offered. "I don't think your car will be ready by then."

He was right. "Okay, that works." She slid out of the passenger seat, then glanced at him over her shoulder. "You heading out?"

"Yeah, I have an appointment at noon." His smile didn't quite reach his eyes. "I'll see you later this evening, okay?"

"Sure." She stepped back and shut the door. It wasn't until she was back in her apartment that she figured out what was bothering her.

Holt hadn't asked her to lunch. Not that he was obligated to feed her every single meal, but his usual pattern was to offer to take her out to lunch or dinner. Or both.

She gave herself a mental shake. Ridiculous to feel slighted that he hadn't asked her to lunch. She didn't need Holt to pay for her meals. Or to spend every waking moment of his day with her.

Deciding on grilled cheese and soup because it was easy and offered a level of comfort, she ate, then tried to nap. Some nurses she worked with could fall asleep on a dime. Unfortunately, she wasn't one of them. But she tried anyway, knowing that even if she rested, doing her deep breathing exercises and clearing her mind, the night would be easier to get through.

To her surprise, she must have dozed because when she opened her eyes it was five o'clock in the evening. She showered and changed into her flight suit, then rummaged in her fridge for something to eat.

When Holt knocked at her door at twenty minutes to seven, she was ready to go. He looked tired but smiled when she came out to greet him.

"Didn't get much sleep?" She glanced at him as they took the stairs down to the basement parking garage.

"No." He shrugged. "But it was worth it, I'll fill you in on the details later."

Details? About what? Curiosity piqued, but she didn't push, knowing it was a short drive to Lifeline's hangar.

When they walked inside, Kate Weber and some resident she didn't know were in the debriefing room.

"Hey, Baxter," the resident greeted Holt. "Get what you needed off the computer?"

"Yeah, thanks." Holt avoided her gaze. "How was your shift?"

"We had several transfers, but nothing too critical." Kate waved a hand. "Drake wanted more drama, but I told him to be glad he didn't need to perform any in-flight heroics."

"I never said I wanted drama." The resident's tone was bland. "I only mentioned needing more experience, that's all."

"You'll get plenty of experience," Holt assured him.

Drake shrugged but didn't say anything more. There was a seriousness in his eyes that made her wonder about his background. Compared to Kate's lightheartedness, he was downright somber.

"No transfers waiting in the wings," Kate went on. "Hopefully you guys will have a quiet night."

"That would be nice," Kristin agreed.

Nate was the oncoming pilot and in deep conversation with Megan. Had she missed something about a turn in the weather? It was known to snow in October, but not this early.

"Something wrong?" she asked Nate as he came over to where they were seated.

"Possible high winds in the forecast, but it's clear now." He didn't look concerned. "I'll keep an eye on the satellite and let you know if anything changes."

"Okay." She waited until both Drake and Kate had left the building before gesturing for Holt to join her in the lounge. "Fill me in. What's going on?"

He dropped onto the sofa and leaned back to look into her eyes. "I had lunch with Paulette and Lana today."

Her heart clenched in her chest, a pang of betrayal hitting hard. "You did?"

"I told them we had evidence that they'd tried to run us off the road, arranged for the teens to throw the baseball at you while jogging, and dumping sugar in your gas tank."

"Proof? We don't have anything remotely close to proof." The bands around her heart loosened as she realized Holt had done this as a way to get them to back off, not because he was interested in rekindling a relationship with Lana.

"They don't know that." His tone was reasonable. "I may have fudged the truth a bit, mentioning that the cops pulled fingerprints off the car and having a photograph of them being at the park together prior to the baseball incident."

She sank onto the corner of the sofa, trying to wrap her mind around what he was telling her. "What did they say?"

"They tried to deny it at first, but I could tell by the way they glanced at each other that they were nervous." Holt hesitated, then added, "I threatened to tell Ben Harris what they'd done."

"Ben Harris?" She searched her memory. "Oh, the Medical Director of the Emergency Department, right?"

Holt nodded. "Yep, and he is not one to put up with any bull. He runs a tight ship and wouldn't look kindly on this kind of crazy retaliation."

"What did they say to that?"

"They tried to bluff, saying if I went to Ben, they'd come after me for defamation of character, but I reminded them we had their fingerprints on the car near the gas tank."

"Nonexistent fingerprints."

"And that if anything else happened to me or to you, in any way, I'd take everything to Dr. Harris and have them kicked out of the program." A wry grin bloomed on his face. "The way they jumped up to leave in a big hurry, whispering together, was priceless. I think they heard the message loud and clear."

"That's good." She let out a sigh, hoping he was right and that this would be the end of the nonsense. "Thanks for doing that, Holt."

"Hey, I told you I'd take care of it. Oh, and I made them pay for the repairs on your car. They agreed and each coughed up five hundred big ones."

"A thousand dollars?" She gaped at the two checks he held out toward her. "We don't even know the repairs will cost that much."

"Doesn't matter. They arranged for you to be hit with a baseball, remember? It's what you deserve."

She took the two checks from his fingers, staring down at them in surprise. "I don't know what to say."

"Say you'll have breakfast with me in the morning when our shift is over." He leaned over to kiss her cheek. "I would have far rather had lunch with you, Kristin."

A blush heated her cheeks. She folded the two checks and tucked them into the pocket of her flight suit. "Okay, breakfast it is."

"Perfect." He looked as if he might kiss her again when their pagers went off.

"It's a trauma call, high-speed motor vehicle crash. They don't have a name, the victim is still pinned in the car, but they're estimating she's young, maybe twenty-six or -seven." It was humbling to realize she would turn twenty-seven herself in November.

"It's always the young ones," Holt muttered as she grabbed the duffel of supplies and led the way through the debriefing room to the landing pad. "So sad."

Nate was waiting near the chopper. "Ready to go?"

She nodded. Holt opened the door and helped her jump up inside. There was a twinge of pain in her right knee, but she ignored it.

They were seated and belted in when Nate finally received the go-ahead from the base to lift off. Once they were in the air, Holt keyed the paramedic base.

"I need an update on the female victim of the motor vehicle crash."

"Ten-four, I'll raise the paramedic on scene." There was a pause before another voice could be heard.

"This is Eli Wentworth, I don't have an update yet as the vic is still in the car. The vehicle flipped over the median and landed upside down on the other side of the freeway. From what we're being told by witnesses, she was speeding at an estimated hundred miles per hour."

Kristin caught her breath. Why on earth would anyone drive that fast? Unless they were under the influence of alcohol or drugs.

"Is she alive?" Holt's blunt question brought her attention back to the conversation.

"As far as we can tell, yes. But we really need to get her extricated from the vehicle."

"Okay, thanks. We'll be there soon." Holt hit the switch, shutting off the all communication button. "Doesn't sound good."

"No, afraid not." She reached over to touch his arm. "We'll do our best to save her."

He smiled and nodded.

"ETA three minutes," Nate said over the radio. "I'm dropping the bird on the interstate."

From her window she could see the car lying on its hood, surrounded by dozens of firefighters and paramedics.

The jaws of life, a large machine that was used to pry open the frame of the automobile, was already in use. She felt certain the victim would be freed by the time they landed.

Nate set the chopper down and gave the all clear for them to disembark. Holt went first, and she followed.

After pulling the gurney out of the hatch, they jogged over to the crash scene. As they came closer, Holt abruptly stopped, his face going white.

"No. Heidi?" His voice was little more than a hoarse croak. "*Heidi!*"

She gaped in surprise as her gaze zeroed in on the victim lying so still on the paramedic's gurney.

Despite the blood and bruises, she could easily recognize Holt's sister, Heidi. As she ran toward the gurney, she was horrified that Holt would be forced to treat his own sister as a trauma patient.

14

He'd never called her back or gone to see *Heidi*. He'd promised his sister he'd drive out to visit but hadn't called her.

Swallowing hard against the bitter self-recriminations flashing in the back of his mind, Holt forced himself to focus on saving Heidi's life. His hands trembled as he pulled his stethoscope from around his neck and listened to his sister's heart and lungs.

But it wasn't easy to concentrate, because deep down, he knew this wasn't a terrible accident. No, if Heidi was going a hundred miles per hour, he knew it was a desperate attempt to end her life.

Not just a cry for help, the way her previous attempt had been, but something far more serious.

"We're losing her pulse." Kristin's voice brought him back to the present. "Possible PE or cardiac tamponade based on the crash."

"Cardiac tamponade, her heart tones are muffled." He glanced up at Kristin. "I need a cardiac needle and fifty cc syringe to release the pressure around her heart."

Kristin's expression was full of concern as she pulled the necessary equipment from her duffel bag. He prepped Heidi's chest, doing his best not to think of her as his sister but as a patient who needed his expertise.

Drawing a deep breath, he carefully inserted the needle and drew back on the syringe, removing blood from the sac around her heart.

"Pulse is stronger now," Kristin said. "Blood pressure at eighty-eight over thirty-six."

Still too low. The injuries Heidi had suffered were staggering, but he did his best to prioritize the damage to her heart, her lungs, and her brain.

He checked her pupils, which were slightly unequal but still reactive. Her lung sounds were diminished in the bases, and he felt certain she had bilaterally pneumothoraxes. "I need two chest tubes. Start a Mannitol drip."

"She's already hypotensive," Kristin said in a mild tone. "Might be better to hold off for a bit."

"Her pupils are unequal." As he prepped the right side of her chest, he tried not to panic. Was Mannitol the right thing to do? Or was Kristin right about waiting? When Kristin handed him the first chest tube, he deftly inserted it, his stomach clenching with horror when blood poured out.

"Hemothorax, she's bleeding from her lungs! We need to get her on the chopper and to Trinity ASAP."

Kristin's voice sounded faint, as if she were standing on the other end of a long tunnel. Sweat dampened his temples and pooled in the small of his back.

They were losing her.

"Fluids are wide open." Kristin's voice was louder now. "I have two units of O neg blood."

"Give them, and let's get her onto our gurney." He knew

that Heidi could bleed to death if they didn't replace what she was losing from the chest tube.

The entire paramedic team stayed to help them stabilize his sister. Within moments, they had two IVs going with blood and fluids running simultaneously. They transferred Heidi to the Lifeline gurney and covered her with a heavy blanket to help prevent her from going into full-blown shock.

Kristin pushed the gurney, forcing him to move quickly. Together they lifted Heidi through the hatch, then he held the gurney steady as Kristin ran around to pull her the rest of the way in.

"Nate? We're ready," Kristin said.

Holt busied himself with placing the second chest tube on the left side of his sister's chest. She didn't flinch beneath the prick of the needle, and he couldn't decide if that was a good sign or bad one.

Thankfully, no blood came through the chest tube on this side, and while he couldn't hear the rush of air coming out from the opening, her blood pressure went up to 94/48.

He felt encouraged by her response and prayed she'd make it.

Don't you die on me, Heidi. Not today, understand. Fight! You need to fight for your life! You don't really want to die. I know, deep down, you really don't want to die!

"Her vitals are hanging in there," Kristin said. "Nate, we're going to need a hot unload. We need a cardiothoracic surgeon and the trauma team waiting for us."

Holt realized he should have been the one making arrangements and pulled himself together with an effort. He listened to her heart and lungs again, disturbed by the muffled heart tones again. "More blood is building up around her heart. I need another syringe." He'd kept the needle embedded from the original procedure, having learned the hard way on a previous patient that it was common to have blood building up around the heart more than once.

Time dragged by as if in slow motion. He knew it was only a ten-minute flight, but it seemed three times as long considering his sister's life was hanging in the balance.

All because he hadn't gone to see her. Instead, he'd taken care of things for Kristin, putting her needs ahead of his family.

Nate banked the chopper, indicating they were about to land. The second the helicopter came to rest, he pushed open his door and ran around to pull Heidi from the back.

As promised, a full team waited for them just inside the building. Holt couldn't seem to find his voice, but Kristin quickly filled them in on Heidi's condition.

"We'll take it from here," the ED attending said, putting a hand on Holt's shoulder.

He shrugged it off. "I'm coming with you."

"Not into the OR you aren't." The surgeon was an older guy who'd been around for a while.

Holt knew he wasn't allowed to watch them operate on Heidi, but he couldn't tear himself away. He and Kristin walked alongside as they pushed the gurney to the operating room. After they'd transferred Heidi onto the OR table and disconnected the equipment, they left.

In the corridor outside the OR suite, he suddenly stopped, realization hitting hard. "I need to call my parents."

Kristin hesitated, then nodded. "You stay here and call your parents. I'll take our stuff back to the chopper. I'll find someone to cover your shift."

He nodded, barely hearing what she was saying, his gaze locked on the cell phone he held in his hand. He pushed the button for his father's cell phone and lifted the device to his ear.

What should he tell them? That Heidi was driving one hundred miles per hour and crashed her car in what he believed was another suicide attempt?

And worse, that it was likely his fault for breaking his promise to call her? To go out and visit her?

He sank to the hard linoleum floor and dropped his head between his knees. If his sister didn't make it, he'd have no one to blame but himself.

KRISTIN CALLED Jared the minute she and Nate returned to the Lifeline hangar, filling him in on Holt's sister's condition and the fact that she needed another physician to fill in the rest of his shift.

"I'll be right there," Jared promised.

She let out a sigh of relief and began the mundane tasks of cleaning blood from the gurney and restocking supplies. But her mind kept whirling about Heidi's crash.

Holt's sister had been her nemesis in high school, but now she could only feel sorry for the woman. After graduating from college and beginning her career as a nurse, she'd never given Heidi another thought, at least not until Holt had walked back into her life.

Even then, she'd just assumed Heidi was as accomplished as Holt, either working in some high-powered job or married to a man with a high-powered job. Why on earth had she been driving along the interstate at high speed?

Holt shouldn't be dealing with this alone. But as much as she wanted to be there for him, she couldn't walk out on her shift. When Jared arrived a few minutes later, she filled him in on the details.

"Holt's in rough shape, he had to do a pericardial tap and place two chest tubes. She had a hemothorax on the right and a pneumothorax on the left."

Jared scrubbed a hand over his face. "On his own sister."

"Yeah." She drew in a deep breath and let it out slowly. "He was calling his parents when I left, but I feel bad that he's there all alone."

"Any transfers pending?" Jared asked.

"No."

"Go back to Trinity to check on Holt. It's not far, you can be back soon enough if we get a call."

"Thanks." Relieved he was being so understanding, she hurried out of the hangar, picking up her pace to a light jog to get back to the hospital.

She looked for Holt in the family center and the surgical waiting area without success. When she returned to the hallway where she'd left him, she found him sitting on the floor in the same spot where she'd left him, his arms crossed on his knees, his head down.

"Holt? Why don't we head down to the family center?"

He lifted his head, his eyes red and watery. Her heart squeezed when he realized he'd been crying. "I'm fine. Go back to Lifeline."

She was taken aback by his tone but knew he was probably embarrassed to be caught in such a vulnerable position. "Come on, Holt. You can't stay here. The surgeon will head down to the family center when he's finished."

She put a hand under Holt's arm, but he shrugged her off and then slowly rose to his feet. "I'm fine," he repeated. "My parents will be here soon. Just go back to work."

There was no mistaking the dismissal in his tone. "What's wrong? Are you mad at me about something?"

He shook his head without meeting her gaze. "I—just need to be alone. I can't deal with you right now."

"Okay." She stepped back, trying not to feel hurt. She'd thought they were closer than this, that he'd lean on her in times of stress, the way she'd leaned on him.

Apparently not.

Worse, he was acting as if he didn't want anything to do with her.

Kristin walked back to the Lifeline hangar with a strange sense of loss.

The relationship that she'd imagined growing between them was nothing more than a figment of her imagination.

This was exactly what she'd been afraid of all along.

That Holt Baxter would break her heart.

CONSUMED with guilt over his sister's crash, Holt barely noticed when Kristin left. He knew he'd been rude, but he didn't care. His feelings for Kristin were what caused this mess, he deserved to feel lousy.

Kristin didn't deserve it, but the all-consuming guilt wouldn't stop eating at him. There was no way he could tolerate having her beside him while he waited to hear if Heidi would live or die.

And if she lived, what her condition might be. Would she recover fully or end up in a comatose state for some unknown period of time? Head injuries were serious. Even if she survived surgery, she might not wake up. And if she did wake up, she might be paralyzed on one side from the head injury. He squeezed his eyes shut as if he could erase the image forming in his mind.

His parents arrived wearing somber expressions as they sat beside him in the family center. Even his mother was subdued as his father asked for an update.

"I haven't heard anything." He forced himself to look at his father. "But I don't think this was an accident. I think she was driving at a high rate of speed on purpose."

"You don't know that," his mother snapped.

"Stop ignoring the truth staring you in the face," he shot back. "Heidi has been a mess for the past year since her divorce. You know it, I know it, and this isn't the first time she's tried to hurt herself."

"Okay, son, you've made your point." His dad, ever the peacemaker, spoke in a soothing tone. "When Heidi gets out of the hospital, we'll convince her to get the counseling she needs."

If she makes it out of surgery, the traitorous part of his brain said. *Not when, if.*

"Meds too," he said. "Antidepressants."

His mother looked as if she might argue, but his father quickly interjected. "Of course. Heidi clearly needs help, and we'll all be there for her."

Yeah. Everyone except for him.

Three hours later the surgeon finally walked into the family center. When he saw Holt, he crossed over. "Dr. Baxter?"

"Yes. These are my parents. How is she?"

"I was able to repair the laceration in her heart and stop the bleeding into her right lung. She's recovering now and will be admitted to the ICU very soon."

"What about her neuro status?" He forced himself to

meet the surgeon's gaze. "Her pupils were unequal in the field, indicating brain trauma."

"We've consulted neurosurgery, they'll be watching for any brain swelling. I think they're planning to do a CT scan of her head, and the rest of her internal organs, once she's stabilized in the ICU."

Hope flickered deep in his heart, even though he knew it was far too early to call this a success.

"There may be other fractures," the surgeon cautioned. "We haven't had time to do a full body exam. We'll know more after the CT scan."

"Understood. Thanks." Holt felt dizzy with relief. Not that Heidi was out of the woods, but she was alive.

And if anyone could keep her that way, it was Trinity's trauma team.

He closed his eyes and thanked God for watching over his sister.

KRISTIN DIDN'T SEE Holt for an agonizing two full days. She'd called the hospital for updates, encouraged by the news but hadn't wanted to intrude. On her day off, she decided enough was enough. She would show up at Heidi's bedside and see for herself how Holt was holding up.

Before she could leave her apartment, there was a knock at her door. She was surprised to find Holt standing there, looking ragged, unshaven, and exhausted, but his eyes were clearer than they'd been before.

"How is she?" Kristin opened the door to let him in.

"Better." Holt crossed over to sit on the sofa. "I owe you an apology."

"It's fine." She waved it off, even though she was glad he wasn't still mad at her.

He shook his head, then drew in a deep breath. "Heidi tried to commit suicide once before, and the police believe this recent crash was a second attempt to kill herself."

She'd done it before? Stunned, Kristin sank beside him. "I—don't know what to say."

"She found out her husband was cheating on her, and the scandal and divorce was too much for her to handle." He grimaced. "On the day of the crash, I was supposed to call her, to get together with her. But I towed your car and made lunch arrangements with Lana and Paulette instead."

For her. "I see. You think it's your fault she took a reckless high-speed joy ride that nearly killed her?"

His green eyes sparked with anger. "I told her I'd be there, and I wasn't. That's on me."

"Okay, yes. But did she call you?"

Holt shook his head. "She shouldn't have to. I was supposed to call her and to go over to see her."

"She didn't call you and didn't tell you she was thinking of killing herself, so how were you supposed to know?"

"Because she's done it before." He abruptly stood. "I'm sorry I was rude. I wanted you to understand why I feel so guilty."

She knew he was about to leave and suddenly couldn't stand it. "Holt, please sit down so we can talk this out."

He eyed her warily, then slowly sat. "I know you and Heidi weren't friends."

"You're right, we weren't. She treated me terribly, but that doesn't mean I want to see her hurt like this. Or you being hurt. But I also don't think you should feel responsible for her actions."

He shook his head. "I'm responsible for not following through on my promise."

"But she has to accept the outcome of her choices." No one had held Heidi responsible for the way she'd treated Kristin and some of the other nerdy girls back in high school.

"Depression is an illness."

"You're right, it is. And a big part of that illness makes it nearly impossible for her to appreciate the impact of her decisions. Her decisions, not yours."

"Yeah." He sighed. "Which is why I should have been there for her."

"Holt, please don't take all of this on your shoulders. It's not right. What if you had gone to see her but she still made the choice to drive at high rates of speed? Would you feel responsible?"

"Maybe not." He hung his head for a long moment. "I guess there's a part of me that feels bad that I was so happy spending time with you when she was so miserable."

His words touched her heart. "I'm sorry she's miserable, Holt, and no one deserves to be cheated on. Who did she marry?"

"Trent Olson."

"From high school?" Even as the words left her mouth, she realized Holt Baxter, her crush from high school, was sitting right beside her. Talk about irony.

"Yeah, they married too young, right after they graduated from college." His gaze sought hers. "You may be right about her decisions, she needs to own them, but she's had it tough this past year."

It would be petty to point out that Kristin had gone through worse in high school dealing with Heidi's taunts, so she didn't say anything. Especially since whatever hold

Heidi had held over her back then was long gone. She was in a much better place than Heidi. "I know, I went through the whole cheating thing with Greg. Thankfully we weren't married, but still."

He surprised her by reaching out to take her hand. "I admire your ability to handle stress, personally and professionally."

"I have my bad days, too." He was making her sound like some sort of superwoman, which was far from the truth.

"I've missed you, Kristin. I pushed you away when I needed you the most. I haven't been able to stop thinking about you, even as I was battling guilt."

"It's okay, Holt." She couldn't deny she was glad to see him. "Finding your sister as the victim of a crash had to be difficult. I can't even imagine how you were able to take care of her the way you did."

"Yeah, but that wasn't the worst part." Holt hesitated, squeezed her hand, and added, "After I chased you away and dealt with my parents, I was suddenly scared to death that I'd lost the best thing that has ever happened to me."

She frowned. "You won't lose your position at Lifeline. Jared completely understands what you've been going through."

"Not that, silly. You." He tugged on her hand and drew her close. "I love you, Kristin. I know it's only been a couple of weeks, but the moment I saw you in the Lifeline hangar I knew you'd change my life. And you have, for the better. I love you, and I don't want to lose you. Will you please forgive me?"

"Love?" Her mind could barely grasp what he was telling her. "Love? Are you sure?"

A cautious expression flickered over his features. "I'm sure, Kristin. I was attracted to you back in high school, and even more so now that I've gotten to know you. But if it's too soon for you, I understand. We can take things slow as long as you give me a chance to prove how much I care about you."

Bemused, she looked up into his earnest expression, and the walls surrounding her heart crashed to the floor. "Holt, I had a crush on you back in high school, and now that I've gotten to know you better, my feelings for you have blossomed and grown. It has been quick, but honestly? I love you, too."

"Alleluia." He pulled her close and covered her mouth with a deep kiss.

She reveled in his embrace, clinging to his shoulders so she wouldn't fall down as she kissed him back.

"I won't let you down," he murmured when they could both speak.

"Holt, nothing is perfect in the world, as we both know. We're bound to make mistakes along the way, so don't focus on the occasional missteps. Just know our love will see us through."

He nodded and rested his forehead against hers. "You're right, so how about I promise to never stop loving you no matter what?"

She couldn't help but smile. "And I promise to love you, too, no matter what."

He kissed her again, then straightened. "We'd better get going."

She leaned back. "Where?"

"To the hospital. I think it's time for you to meet my parents."

"Wait, what? Now? I don't think ..."

"Shh." He touched her lips with his fingertip. "I love you, Kristin, just the way you are. And they will, too."

She wasn't sure she was ready for this and tried one more time. "What about Heidi? She's probably not ready."

"She woke up earlier this morning, and I told her all about you. About us. Or at least the us I was hoping for." His smile was crooked. "Will you please come with me?"

Looking up into his mesmerizing green gaze, she knew it would be impossible to refuse. "All right. Let's go."

"I love you." His gaze was seriously intense.

"And I love you, too." She put her hand in his, knowing this was the start of a new beginning.

EPILOGUE

F*our weeks later...*

Holt patted the pocket of his leather jacket, reassuring himself that the ring was still there. He'd made reservations at a very nice restaurant located close to the hospital and just had to pick up Kristin who was visiting Heidi.

When he arrived up on the rehab unit, he was surprised to see Heidi was walking in the hallway with her crutches. She'd fractured her left leg, which was still in an immobilizer. Earlier in the day her doctor had granted her permission to do some weight-bearing.

"Look at you. Good going, sis."

"Yeah, I'm a rock star." Her deadpan voice indicated just the opposite, but he ignored her tone. Heidi had faced some tough challenges over the past four weeks, recovering from her heart and lung surgery and getting her strength back while dealing with a fractured leg and several rib fractures. Her head injury had proved minor, likely thanks to the airbag and the fact that she was wearing her seat belt. The best thing about being in the hospital for this long were the daily visits from the trauma psychiatrist.

"It's your ticket to getting home, remember?" Kristin was walking alongside her. "That's your goal, right?"

"Right." Heidi gritted her teeth and took another step. "Anything to get away from this torture."

It had taken Holt a few weeks to realize that Heidi's somewhat fatalistic attitude would never change. It was something she'd inherited from their mother, and while he wanted to support his sister, he also needed to hold her responsible for her actions.

"Another ten feet and we can turn around and go back to your room," Kristin said.

Heidi didn't protest, probably because she knew it would be useless. It was difficult to watch her struggle, but he was also glad to see her up and moving.

"Where are you guys going for dinner?" Heidi paused at the halfway point and painstakingly turned around for the return trip to her room.

"Fosters, it's that new steak place." He glanced at Kristin, wondering if she suspected this was a special occasion.

"Ooh, expensive," Heidi said.

Kristin's eyes widened with alarm. "Nothing fancy," he assured her. "Don't worry." He shot Heidi a look that told her to shut up.

When Heidi finally made it back to her room, she eased into the chair with a sigh. He took her crutches and set them nearby. "Pretty sad that I'm worn out after a measly walk up and down the hallway."

"Focus on the positive, you've come a long way," Kristin said.

Heidi nodded. "I'm trying."

"We'd better get going, our reservation is for seven."

"Have fun." Heidi forced a smile

"We will." He stepped to the side, allowing Kristin to go first.

"Kristin?" Heidi's voice stopped her.

"Yes?" Kristin glanced at his sister. "Do you need something?"

"No, but um, thank you for being here over these past few weeks. I shouldn't have been so mean to you in high school."

He felt Kristin stiffen, but she merely nodded. "It's okay, that's all in the past."

Heidi didn't respond for a minute, then added, "It was stupid of me to consider myself better than everyone else. Look at how you turned out to be smarter and more successful than I'll ever be."

Kristin smiled and went over to give Heidi a hug. "Stop comparing yourself to others and you'll find you're just as smart and successful in your own way. Everyone has their own path, you just need to find yours."

"You think so?" His sister's eyes were full of hope.

"Absolutely. Take care, Heidi. I'll see you tomorrow."

Holt put his arm around her shoulders as they walked out of the hospital to his truck. "You're one amazing lady, Kristin."

"And you're lucky to have me," she teased, playfully elbowing him in the side.

"True." He patted the ring again before sliding into the driver's seat.

The restaurant was everything he'd hoped for, nice and quiet with lit candles in the center of the table. After they ordered soft drinks and appetizers, he decided it was now or never.

He got out of his chair and then knelt at her side. She looked puzzled, until she caught a glimpse of the ring.

"Kristin, will you please marry me?"

"Oh, Holt." Her eyes misted, but her face radiated with joy. "Yes, of course I'll marry you."

"I love you." He slipped the ring onto the fourth finger of her left hand, then drew her to her feet to kiss her.

The patrons around them burst into applause, making her blush.

"You're embarrassing me."

"Being engaged to me is embarrassing?" His teasing tone lightened the mood. But as they took their seats, his expression turned serious. "I'll never cheat on you, Kristin."

"I know. And I'll never cheat on you either."

He glanced down at their entwined hands and knew she'd be the best partner and wife he could ever ask for.

And silently vowed to be the same for her.

DEAR READER

I hope you enjoyed *A Doctor's Reunion*, the fifth book in my Lifeline Air Rescue series. This book deals with two serious and difficult subjects, bullying and depression, and while this book is a romance, I fully appreciate there is not always a happy ending. My heart goes out to anyone touched by these difficult situations.

As a Registered Nurse by day and an author by night, I was fortunate enough to do a ride along in our very own Flight For Life. I found the challenges of providing patient care miles up in the air fascinating. One twelve-hour shift and this series was born.

Reviews are very important to authors, so please consider leaving a review on the platform from which you purchased the book. I adore hearing from my readers and can be contacted through my website https://laurascottbooks.com. All newsletter subscribers are offered a free novella, a story not available for sale on any platform, so if you're interested, please sign up via my website. I can also be found on Facebook https://www.facebook.com/

LauraScottBooks/ and Twitter https:// twitter.com/laurascottbooks.

Yours in faith,

Laura Scott

PS. If you're interested in reading another series, please check out my McNally Family series. The first chapter of *To Love* is included here.

TO LOVE

Several loud thuds woke Jazzlyn McNally up from a sound sleep. For a minute, she thought the noise had been something she'd dreamed, then she heard it again. Louder. She wasn't sure, but it almost sounded as if several two-by-fours were being dropped.

What in the world?

She rolled out of bed, tugging her oversized T-shirt down over her gym shorts, and headed downstairs, wincing as one of the wooden boards creaked beneath her bare feet. What if the noise was from somewhere inside the house? She reached the bottom of the stairs, flattened herself against the wall, then gingerly peered around the corner, looking into the great room.

Casting her gaze over the main living area, the fireplace, the lighthouse oil painting over the mantle, and the antique glossy cherrywood furniture, nothing seemed out of place. But she knew she hadn't imagined the sounds, so as she made her way through her grandparents' old mansion, she picked up a claw hammer to use as a possible weapon.

Everything was fine inside the house, but when she

walked over to the French doors overlooking Lake Michigan, she noticed several boards strewn across the lawn.

Her gazebo!

Sick to her stomach, Jazz flung open the doors and stumbled outside.

No! It couldn't be! Two sections of the gazebo she'd worked on for the past three days had been destroyed in one fell swoop. She stared in horror, her mind trying to comprehend what had happened. Vandals had struck. In fact, the sledgehammer they'd used was still lying in the center of the destruction.

But who would do such a thing? And why?

In the early morning light, she could see the area was deserted. Whoever had done this was long gone. Maybe in the time it took her to go through the house. It was difficult to tear her gaze away from the damaged remnants of her hard work.

She shivered in the crisp April breeze coming off the lake. Drawing a deep shuddering breath, she turned and went back inside to find her cell phone. She called the Clark County Sheriff's Department for the second time in a week.

The first incident, a broken window in the front door, had been bad enough.

But this? Destroying two sections of the gazebo she'd recently repaired? This time, the vandals had gone too far.

"Clark County Sheriff's Department," the female dispatcher answered. "How can I help you?"

"This is Jazzlyn McNally, and I need a deputy here ASAP. The vandals have used my sledgehammer to wreck my gazebo; it's lying in pieces across my lawn."

"I'll send a deputy," the dispatcher responded. The

woman didn't ask for her address; the entire town knew where the McNally Mansion was located.

"Thank you." Jazz disconnected from the call and combed her fingers through her disheveled hair, her inner fury subsiding to a dull resignation. Even if the police found who'd done this, she would still need to fix everything that had been destroyed. At this rate, her goal of opening the B&B before Memorial Day wasn't going to happen.

She gave herself a mental shake, knowing she needed to remain positive. She could do this. How much time before the deputy arrived? She figured she had ten minutes at the most, so she ran upstairs to the green room, her favorite, to change into a sweatshirt and jeans.

Five minutes later, Jazz returned to the kitchen to brew a pot of coffee. The scent helped her to relax a bit, and she poured a cup, grateful for the jolt of caffeine.

But when the deputy still hadn't arrived by the time she'd finished two cups of coffee, her anger began to simmer. By eight o'clock in the morning, she tapped her foot on the floor, wondering how long it would take for someone to arrive.

Apparently, vandalism of personal property wasn't high on the Clark County Sheriff's list of priorities.

Another hour passed. A knock at the front door made her frown. She hadn't heard a car come up the driveway. Setting her coffee aside, she reached for her claw hammer and made her way to the newly repaired front door. She peeked through the recently replaced window.

A man roughly six feet tall with longish dark hair stood there, wearing a threadbare red and gray checkered flannel shirt, faded black jeans, and construction boots.

Not the deputy.

The vandal? But why knock at her door?

She hesitated so long he rapped again, a little louder this time. The stranger hunched his shoulders and rubbed his hands together as if he were cold. No car meant he'd either walked or hitchhiked from town.

Against her better judgment, she opened the door still holding the claw hammer in clear view as she eyed him with suspicion. "Yes?"

The stranger smiled, but it didn't reach his dark eyes. "Ms. McNally? My name is Dalton O'Brien, and I was told by Stuart Sewell from the hardware store that you might be looking for some construction help. I work hard and accept cash if you're interested."

Jazz stared at him for a long moment, wondering if this guy was really brazen enough to destroy her gazebo, then come back to ask to be paid to fix it. "How did you get here?"

He looked surprised at her question. "I hitched a ride from the Pine Cone Campsite. The driver let me out on Main Street, so I walked from there."

The Pine Cone Campsite was over twenty miles from the center of town. If he was being honest, then he probably wasn't her vandal.

Still, she didn't like the timing of his arrival.

"I can provide references if needed," O'Brien went on. "I did some work on Mrs. Cromwell's bathroom a week ago."

Jazz knew Betty Cromwell. Everyone in town knew Betty, the woman was one of the biggest sources of gossip in McNally Bay. If Betty would vouch for this guy, she may be interested.

She was just about to ask for his contact information when a dark brown sedan pulled in, the words Clark County Sheriff's Department etched along the side. Finally!

Dalton O'Brien turned to watch the cop car approach,

not looking the least bit nervous as he tucked his hands into the front pockets of his jeans.

Trusting her instincts wasn't easy. Jazz had learned the hard way that she was too naïve when it came to trusting men. Yet for some reason, she didn't think the handsome stranger was the person who'd vandalized her gazebo.

Or maybe she just didn't want to believe it.

"Ma'am, I'm Deputy Garth Lewis. I understand you've had more trouble this morning?"

"Yes." Jazz opened the door wider and gestured with her hand. "Come in, both of you. I have fresh coffee if you're interested."

Both Dalton and Deputy Lewis glanced around with interest. While she loved the beautiful great room, she led the way into the kitchen and pulled two coffee mugs out of the cabinet.

"O'Brien," Deputy Lewis said with a nod. "Are you here looking for work?"

"Yes, sir." Dalton didn't say anything more, and the two men stood awkwardly in the large kitchen.

It was reassuring that the deputy knew Dalton O'Brien by name. She handed them both steaming mugs of coffee. "Cream or sugar?"

"Black is fine," Deputy Lewis said.

"For me, too," Dalton added.

"Okay then. Mr. O'Brien, why don't you have a seat for a moment while I talk to the deputy?" She crossed over to the French doors, opened them, and then stepped back so the deputy could see the vandalism for himself.

Deputy Lewis let out a low whistle. "When did this happen?"

She crossed her arms over her Michigan State sweatshirt. "The noise woke me up at six this morning. I went through the house first, so I didn't see the damage out here right away. By the time I did, whoever had done this was long gone."

The deputy met her gaze. "I saw your report about the damaged front door and now this. Do you have any enemies that we need to know about?"

"None that I'm aware of." Jazz glanced at the stranger who'd come over to see the vandalism for himself. Then she turned back to the deputy. "You probably know this house belonged to my grandparents, Jerry and Joan McNally. Our family has lived here in Clark County for a hundred and fifty years, since our great-great-grandparents immigrated from Ireland. The bay was named after them."

"I'm well aware of the town history," Deputy Lewis said in a dry tone.

She gestured to the interior of the large Victorian house that she was in the process of turning into The McNallys' B&B. "My siblings and I only spent summers here, until our grandma passed away, willing the property to us. You'd know more about any possible enemies than I would."

"What's the approximate cost of the damage?" Deputy Lewis asked as he pulled out a small notepad and stubby pencil.

"Around two grand," the stranger said. "Maybe less, depending on how much of the lumber can be salvaged."

She stared at him in surprise. "That's exactly what I would have estimated," she murmured. "I guess you know your way around construction sites."

O'Brien gave a curt nod. "I do."

"Well then." Jazz let out her breath in a heavy sigh. "I guess I could use a little help, if you're willing."

The stranger nodded and took another sip of his coffee.

Jazz waited for Deputy Lewis to finish his report, which included taking pictures of the crime scene. He also bagged the sledgehammer, on the off chance he might be able to lift some fingerprints from the wooden handle. The deputy left, promising to be in touch if he had any news. Afterward, she returned to the kitchen, the stranger following like her shadow.

"You hungry?" she asked.

His eyes flared with hope. "Yes, ma'am."

"Please call me Jazz, ma'am makes me feel old. Veggie omelets okay?"

"I'm not picky," he said in a wry tone.

"Good." Jazz opened the fridge and pulled out a carton of eggs and the veggies—broccoli, onions, and mushrooms that were left over from the night before. "After breakfast, we'll get to work."

He nodded again without saying anything more.

A man of few words, she thought, his dark eyes shadowed with secrets. She told herself it didn't matter why he was hitching rides and living in a campsite. Not her business one way or the other.

Jazz only needed his assistance for the next couple of weeks, then he could be on his way. Fine with her, because she didn't need any complications in her life.

Or distractions.

~

In Dalton's opinion, the veggie omelet Jazz had made for him was the best he'd ever tasted, but as usual, he kept his thoughts to himself.

He was only here to make a few extra bucks before moving on. His plan was to head further north, knowing that construction jobs would be plentiful there during the summer months.

The damage to the gazebo made him mad, especially the way Jazz had looked so devastated at the senseless destruction.

Ms. McNally, he sternly reminded himself. Okay, yeah, she was beautiful with her long dark brown hair tousled from sleep, and her petite, curvy figure. The way she'd answered the door holding a claw hammer had made him smile, the image still burned into his memory. Beauty aside, he had no intention of crossing the line between employer and employee.

He was a drifter. As soon as this job was finished, he'd be on his way.

Truthfully, he was happy to help. He hated the idea of a young woman living in this huge rambling house alone while vandals went to town on her gazebo.

It wasn't right. He didn't know anything about the McNally legacy, since he'd only been in town for a couple of weeks now, but he had to agree with the deputy that the culprit must be someone holding a grudge against the family.

Which meant just about anyone in town could be considered a possible suspect.

Dalton finished his second cup of coffee, then carried his dirty dishes to the sink. "Thanks for breakfast," he said, then headed outside to see what he could salvage from the wreckage.

Not expecting to be put to work right away, Dalton had left his tool belt at the Pine Cone Campsite. He considered asking Jazz to drive him over there, then figured she probably had enough tools here for him to use.

By the time Jazz joined him, he'd picked through the

entire pile. The lumber he'd stacked together on the right side of the gazebo was good enough to be used again; the left side held the lumber split beyond repair.

"That's better than I'd hoped. This could come in closer to a thousand to repair, excluding labor."

"Agreed. If you're willing loan me tools, I'll begin construction."

"I don't have extras," Jazz said, her expression full of apology. "But you can use anything I have while I head out to buy more lumber."

"Or, if you don't mind swinging past the Pine Cone Campsite, I can pick up my tools," he offered. "We can get the lumber on the way back. With both of us working, we'll get this repaired in no time."

For the first time since he'd arrived, she broke into a wide smile. "Let's do it."

She was alarmingly stunning when she smiled, and he had to force himself to turn away. What was wrong with him? His wife Debbie and their young son, Davy, have only been gone eleven months, not even a full year. He wasn't about to try replacing them in his heart.

Not now. Not ever.

He followed Jazz through the old Victorian house to the circle drive out front. He hadn't paid much attention to the three-car garage, painted yellow with white trim to match the large house, but that's where Jazz headed.

Pushing numbers into a keypad, she stood and waited for the garage door to open. He wasn't sure why he expected to see a small compact car instead of the large bright blue Chevy pickup truck.

"Nice," he said, his tone full of appreciation. As soon as the words left his lips, he frowned. He didn't need a truck, or any other flashy items. That was part of a life he'd left behind and had no interest in returning to. All he needed was a tent, backpack, sleeping bag, and his tools.

"Thanks." Jazz didn't seem to notice anything amiss. She waited till he was seated beside her, before heading out of the garage, closing the door with the push of a button.

The ride to the campground didn't take long. Jazz followed his directions as he told her where to find his camping spot. The red tent was right where he'd left it. He slid out of the passenger seat and went over to unzip the front flap. His backpack, camping gear, and tools were tucked inside.

He emerged a few minutes later to find Jazz standing in front of his tent, regarding it thoughtfully. He lifted his construction tool belt. "I'm ready."

She nodded absently. "Do they charge you a fee to camp here?"

"Yeah, but it's nominal. Why?"

She bit her lower lip for a moment. "How would you feel about camping outside my place instead? It's free, and I'll throw in meals."

He shouldn't have been surprised, but he was. His first instinct was to refuse, he liked her too much already. But then he remembered the vandalism.

It wasn't his problem to keep her property safe. She'd notified the cops who would probably keep a close eye on things. Then again, he knew the deputies couldn't be there all the time. And if the vandals lived in town, they could be at the old Victorian and back within an hour.

"Never mind," Jazz said hastily as if sensing his reluctance. "It's a crazy idea."

Yeah, it was, but he nodded anyway. "I'll do it."

Her green eyes widened in surprise. "You will?"

"Yes. Although we haven't agreed on an hourly wage yet."

She named a fair sum, better than he'd hoped considering she was offering meals, too.

He took a step toward her and held out his hand. "Thank you. I'll take it."

She placed her small, yet slightly calloused hand in his, sending a sliver of awareness down his spine. He did his best to ignore it as they solemnly shook.

"It's a deal." She smiled again, stealing his breath. "I'll help you pack."

"No need, I have a system." He dropped her hand and stepped back, needing distance. He went to work dismantling his campsite with the ease of long practice.

After storing his items in the space behind the bench seat, he climbed in beside her, hoping he wasn't making a huge mistake.

Printed in the USA
CPSIA information can be obtained
at www.ICGtesting.com
LVHW060315140823
755157LV00011B/576